Other Books by Lyn D. Jackson

The Evil Magic of the Blue Dragon Tree

A Very Grave Yarn

The Blood Soaked Trail of Franco De Angelo:
Another Case for Bland and Boyd

The Perilous Journey Home

MURDER MOST BEAUTIFUL

BEAUTIFUL

Bland's last Case?

Lyn D Jackson

authorHOUSE®

AuthorHouse™ UK Ltd.
500 Avebury Boulevard
Central Milton Keynes, MK9 2BE
www.authorhouse.co.uk
Phone: 08001974150

First published by AuthorHouse   1/25/2010

ISBN: 978-1-4490-6807-3 (sc)

This book is printed on acid-free paper.

Forward

Some of my readers did not like the idea that I was going to kill off one of the main characters and requested me not to do so. I can only say to my friends Elaine and Colin, and my dear brother Chas, and our lovely daughter-in-law Sue, that I have noted your comments. . . . .

Chapter One
The Galleries

Teddy and Arthur were moving a large antique bow fronted chest of drawers into the front window of their shop. They were brothers in their sixties, and this was their new venture

Teddy had bought three newly built units, and they were getting ready for their grand opening. The end one, on the corner of the street, was doubled sized, and one half was an artist's studio, and the other half was a gallery, where his work was shown

The artist Steve was in a wheelchair, and had one crushed arm. He had been in an accident some years before; he had been crushed between two cars and a wall .He had little strength, but his paintings were exquisite, especially his miniatures. He lived in the apartment above the studio, which had been adapted to his needs. Teddy had seen to that.

The second unit belonged to Teddy and his younger brother Arthur. They sold antiques and 'objet d'arte'. The last of the three units Teddy had bought for his ex-wife, Queenie. She sold a very good quality of second hand clothes, mostly vintage pieces. Her old shop, and now her new shop, was a meeting place for the local women. The place was never empty. The three units were known collectively as The Galleries. In a fortnight's time there was to be a Grand Opening.

Teddy and Arthur gently lowered the chest of drawers onto a raised dais in the window. It was just high enough so that people looking through the window could get a good view of it without craning their necks.

Hovering behind them was Quentin, Queenie's nephew. He was in his mid thirties and had been employed as their window dresser, for all three properties. He was slim and angular, and was dressed in baggy midnight blue silk trousers that came in and fitted tightly around the ankles. His shirt was a daffodil yellow satin, with voluminous sleeves that came into long tight buttoned cuffs at the wrists. He was sporting a pair of star-shaped sunglasses with diamante all around the edges. His dark hair was cropped and gelled.

"Uncle Teddy," he said, "just an inch to the right." They moved the chest and set it down again.

"Perfect," he said clapping his hands lightly, "now I think we need a roll of purple silk and a golden orb," and he disappeared into the back of the shop.

"Where does he get off calling me Uncle Teddy, I'm not his uncle and he's no blood relation to me."

"He's Queenie's nephew," pointed out Arthur

"True he's Queenie's sister's boy which has nothing to do with me as we is divorced," said Teddy crossly, "added to which he's getting on my tits."

"He does a good job Teddy, look how he arranged the art studio and gallery. It looks like one of them posh places up west."

"And why not?" said Teddy, our Steve is a genius, still as you say Quentin does know 'is business, Queenie's shop looks a fair treat. You wouldn't think that glass; chrome and mirrors could make such a difference.

"A lot is to do wiv lighting," said Arthur, "he's a whiz at that."

"Yes," said Teddy grudgingly, "I suppose your right, but what is he wearing. He looks like something out of the Arabian Nights."

"It's the artistic temperament," said Arthur. Just at that moment Quentin came back, he opened the drawers of the chest and dropped a roll of purple silk in the top one, then he pulled it out so that it dropped in every drawer, finishing in a crushed rosette on the floor by the foot. He then placed a golden orb ornament on top of the chest. The effect was amazing. He adjusted the light and the silk looked like a shiny waterfall cascading from drawer to drawer. The wood looked wonderful, it seemed to glow with golden light.

"There," he said purveying his work, "What do you think?"

"Bloody marvellous," said Teddy, "What else do you plan to go in the window?"

"Well," said Quentin looking around slowly, "a large green palm there in that corner, a painting here, that little French chair you brought up this morning over there, a tall vase of flowers there and that little Victorian work basket just here."

"Is that it?" said Arthur, "you've got bags of room."

"It's just to wet their appetite," said Quentin, "Make them come in for more, Too much only confuses people."

"You're right," said Teddy, "we'll leave you to get on with things."

"Ain't you going to put prices on things" asked Arthur. Quentin looked at him in horror.

"Of course not," he said, "this is a gallery not a shop. It's so high street-chain store putting prices in the window. People who shop here will not worry about the price as they are buying the best that money can buy. If they have to ask the price then they can't afford it. There might of course be negotiated prices for several large purchases."

"Oh I get yer," said Arthur smiling, "a bit of discount off for cash money and no questions asked."

"Certainly not," said Quentin and he flounced out.

"Look Arfer, none of the best shops show their prices, you know that," said Teddy.

"No I don't," said Arthur truculently, "I never shop in them kind of places, the shop assistants always look at you as though you've brought somethin' in on your boots."

"Well," said Teddy, "I'm going up to me allotments."

"I'll join you later," said Arthur, " I'll bring somethin' up for lunch."

"Not corned beef," said Teddy.

"Alright," said Arthur, "not corned beef"

"What are you going to bring then?" said Teddy suspiciously.

"Er – fish and chips" said Arthur hastily

"Good," said Teddy, "and mind you do." Quentin wandered in with a large vase of flowers. He placed them down and viewed them from all angles.

"Not sure," he said.

"Quentin," said Teddy, "I 'ave brought up an old mirror for you to look at. It's in the back of the van. Me and Arthur just dusted it down, it could do wiv a bit of loving care, which I understand is right up your alley, come and have a look at it." They went out into the back yard and Teddy unlocked the van, he pulled back some sacking and revealed a truly old and wonderful Italian mirror.

"Oh," said Quentin clasping his hands together with joy and shivering in delight, "where did you get it?"

"It's an heirloom," said Teddy, "me Dad took it off an broken down Italian prince, in exchange for clearing his debts, back in the twenties. I thought you might like it."

"LIKE IT, LIKE IT, I LOVE IT," cried Quentin, "I'll work on it and we can have it in the gallery on opening day. There is a small Italian crystal chandelier I can put with it."

"Oh joy," he said, "This will be a really grand opening Uncle Teddy"

"Quentin," said Teddy, "just call me Teddy, you don't need to call me uncle"

"Whatever you say, you dear sweet old-fashioned thing," he said brushing imaginary specks off the mirror. Teddy thought it was time to leave, Arthur had already made his escape, and was on his way to the fish and chip shop, Teddy thought he'd go before Quentin in his throes of delight started kissing him, or the mirror, or both.

Chapter Two
A Sweet Oasis of Peace

"Nice and peaceful 'ere isn't it?" said Arthur.

"Yes," said Teddy, "that's one of the reasons I got these allotments."

The allotments were at the top of a large slope, most of which belonged to Teddy. His huts and greenhouses were right at the top. He and his brother were sitting in deck chairs gazing down past the beds of vegetables and flowers. You could see everything from up here, including welcome, or unwelcome visitors as they struggled up the hill.

They were eating their fish and chips, and they had a giant sized jar of pickled onions on the ground between them, which they kept dipping into, spearing the onions with their forks. Behind them was a large barrel of water against the largest shed. They had hung a four-pack of beer on a strap, and it was now cooling in the water.

"Nice bit of fish this," said Arthur.

"You're right Bruv, in that you are not wrong," said Teddy, shaking more vinegar on his chips.

"I've bin 'aving a look round, Arfer."

"At what?" said Arthur.

"At the competition my son, bin looking at antique shops and furniture showrooms."

"And?" queried Arthur

"Ain't nothing to touch us Arfer and the way Quentin is showing the stuff off, or dressing the goods as 'e likes to put it, I think we've got a nice little business here. I've been finking that we ought to pay Quentin more; after all he is looking after three businesses. Maybe he should 'ave an assistant. We've got to look after our end Arfer, Quentin is one of our assets, after all we don't want someone stealing 'im away from us do we?"

"No," said Arthur, "perhaps we should give him a title."

"Like what?" said Teddy.

"'Ow about Artistic Designer for the Galleries? We could put 'im in the brochure."

"Good thinkin' Bruv, that's exactly what we'll do. By the way Frenchie is popping in to see us tomorrow, he's bringing in a few bits of china that he thinks we might be interested in."

"Oh," said Arthur, "Quentin can't stand 'im. Calls 'is antique shop a penny bazaar."

"Really!" said Teddy.

"Yer, said Arthur, "he reckons the shop's full of fairings and factory floor rejects."

"Well," said Teddy, "we'll 'ave to see what Frenchie brings tomorrow – beer Bruv?"

"Don't mind if I do," said Arthur. Teddy got up and took two beers out of the strap and lowered the other two back in the water. He pulled the ring clips and handed one can to his brother.

They settled down, quaffing their beer, and watching the day in peace and quiet.

Chapter Three
Frenchie's Visit

The next morning Teddy and Arthur arrived at the galleries very early, only to find the Quentin had been there most of the night, working on the mirror.

"We really need to replace the gold leaf Uncle Teddy," said Quentin, "most of it has worn off over the years."

"Then do it," said Teddy, "we ain't going to spoil a ship for a ha'p'orth of tar. We want to be known as the best in the business. We won't cut corners, you do what needs to be done Quentin, and while we are on the subject Arfer and I fink you deserve a raise, and we'd like you to be Artistic Designer for the Galleries. You could get yourself an assistant to 'elp you, someone you could train up."

"Yer," said Arthur, "we thought it would be nice if you was featured in the brochure." Teddy and Arthur thought that he might be pleased but were not prepared for the extent of his joy.

"Me," he said, clasping his hands together, Artistic Designer, my picture in the brochure." He grabbed his uncles hugging them both at the same time, planting kisses on the tops of their heads, as he was taller than both of them.

8

"Oh thank-you, thank-you, thank-you," he cried.

"Ere 'ere," said Teddy, "there's no need go bleeding mad."

"My dear uncles, Teddy and Arthur, I love you to bits."

"That's what I'm afraid of," muttered Teddy making sure he was out of Quentin's reach.

"I shall restore this mirror to it former glory, you won't know it. I have a friend who does restorative work. He has a studio in Clerkenwell; he does old clocks and watches mostly, in fact he's just finished an automaton. Perhaps we could take him on as a part time consultant?"

"What ever you say," said Teddy.

"What's an automaton?" said Arthur

"It's a bit like toys for grown ups really," said Quentin, "the one my friend has just finished was about three foot high, a gentleman in Victorian clothes smoking a cigar, and looking through a monocle, and moving his head, He's just started on a lady in a ballet dress, she has a musical box in her base, and when it is wound up she dances."

"Oh," said Arthur.

There was a tap on the window and they turned to see Frenchie peering through the glass, clutching some newspaper parcels.

"Ugh," said Quentin. He whipped open the door and said, "traders go around the back, we do not do business in the salon, it's so vulgar," and he shuddered.

"Don't worry Quentin," said Teddy, "I'll take Frenchie through to the office at the back."

"In that case," said Quentin, "while you are here uncle, I will go and get that gold leaf."

"Take a taxi," said Teddy.

"Thank-you my dear Uncle," he said, and he put on a flowing floor length black cape and swept out of the door.

"Who does he think 'e is?" said Frenchie, "the Phantom of ze Opera?"

9

"Don't mind 'im," said Teddy, "it's 'is artistic temperament. Come into the office at the back." As they went through the workshop Frenchie noticed the mirror.

"Mon Dieu," he said in quiet amazement, "where did you get that mirror, and what do you want for it?"

"Oh the mirror," said Arthur, "we is restoring it for the opening, we is bringing it back to its former glory."

"You need new gold on the frame," said Frenchie, "I suppose you could paint it."

"Paint it, PAINT IT," said Arthur in disgust, forgetting that a couple of hours ago he would have painted it himself, "we ain't doing no botch job. If it needs gold then gold it's going to get, Quentin has just gone out for some gold leaf, he's restoring it."

"What 'im, ze big fairy, what does 'e know?"

"Quentin 'as bin to college and 'as qualifications," said Teddy, "we intend to sell the best of the best; if things need restoring they will be restored by Quentin or one of our uver consultants."

"Well suit yourself, *Mon ami*," said Frenchie shrugging his shoulders in the Gallic manner, and placed his parcels on the table. He started to unwrap them. Frenchie was a short dapper little man. He wore a yellow check waistcoat over his rotund stomach, and tapered trousers of the old style. His pointed neat black patent shoes peeped out from his trousers. He wore an open necked shirt with a green silk cravat around his neck. He sported a sparse ginger moustache, which he was constantly twiddling at the ends to make them into a point. Covering his balding head he wore a French black beret, which he was never seen without.

Teddy and Arthur watched closely as Frenchie laid out about twenty pieces. Teddy began to think that Quentin was right, most of the pieces he wouldn't give a second glance, however there were five pieces he was interested in, a creamery jug, a piece of Missien, two pieces of Coalport and a small piece of Lalique. He only glanced at the pieces he was interested in, he knew how much he was prepared to pay for them, and he didn't want Frenchie to be aware of his interest because he would only push up the price.

Nah," said Teddy, "ain't nuffin 'ere that I'm interested in, what do you fink Arfer?"

"No," said Arthur, "nuffin catches me eye, tell you what I'll go and make some coffee, so your visit ain't been a complete waste," and he disappeared into the kitchen. This was an old tactic of theirs and they knew that Frenchie might think of lowering his prices just to get a sale and not go home empty handed. There was a moment or twos silence and Teddy said,

Look 'ere Frenchie, I feel bad about not 'aving anythin', I'll tell you what I'll do, I'll take those five pieces on the end as a job lot," and he made Frenchie an offer.

"What do you say?"

"They are my best five pieces," wailed Frenchie

"Come off it Frenchie, nobody buys white china anymore, that jug wont sell for a start, and those two pieces are a bit too ornate for my taste, that's not bad," he said pointing to the Coalport, "and that's just a piece of glass."

"It's Lalique you silly Englishman,"

"What ever," said Teddy, and he made his offer again.

"Never," said Frenchie, and then he stated what he wanted for the pieces.

"You must be 'aving a laugh," said Teddy, and he made an offer nearer the price he was willing to pay.

"Done," said Frenchie, "you robbing Englishman," and they spit on their palms and shook hands. Teddy put the pieces in the workshop ready for Quentin to sort out later. He paid Frenchie and helped him to rewrap his remaining pieces. Arthur came in with the tray and placed it on the desk. He poured the coffee and handed it around.

"Bought some bits Arfer," said Teddy.

"Fought you didn't want none," said Arthur.

"Well," said Teddy, "couldn't let an old mate bring 'is stuff down and not buy somefing."

"You a fool to yourself," sighed Arthur.

"He robbed me," exclaimed Frenchie almost choking on his coffee, "best robber in the business because you feel no pain."

Chapter Four
Beth

"Ere," said Arthur, "saw that kid again."

"What kid," said Teddy.

"You know Fanny and Johnny Oates kid."

"You mean Beth?"

"Yer, she is out in the street begging."

"What," said Teddy, "show me. I didn't know that scum bag Johnny Oates was back in town." They all went through the shop and out into the street.

Beth was eight years old, and crippled. She had been born with a withered leg, and unfortunately there was nothing that could be done for her. She was extremely thin and her face looked all eyes. Her wispy blonde hair was cut short and straight, and was dirty and matted. She was dirty, as were her clothes. She was sitting on a filthy blanket with her withered leg exposed. There was an old flat cap on the ground in front of her, to collect money in and she held one small thin hand out to passers by, in the hope that they would put something in the hat.

"Arfer what change 'ave you got in your pocket, and you Frenchie," said Teddy emptying his own. Between them they had fifteen pounds, which

13

Arthur went over and dropped into the hat. When Arthur had walked back to the galleries Johnny Oates appeared, He emptied the hat into his pocket, he clumped Beth around the head and she started to cry, the tears making streaks down her cheeks as they washed away the dirt. He glanced around and disappeared.

"Well," said Arthur, "that'll be spent in the pub at lunchtime. Don't do 'er no good."

"Where's the Social Services," said Teddy.

"They wont find 'im cos he keeps the three of them on the move," said Arthur.

Frenchie excused himself and went down the road, but was soon back with an ice cream which he gave to Beth, and then joined Arthur and Teddy.

"There," he said, "something 'e cant spend in ze public 'ouse"

"There's a flatfoot coming down the road," said Arthur.

"Good," said Teddy, "perhaps they will take her into care."

All at once Johnny was there. He hit Beth in the face, threw away the ice cream, gathered Beth, the blanket and the hat up and disappeared into the crowd.

"Pauvre enfant," said Frenchie.

"Poor little cow," said Teddy.

"Ain't no life for a child," said Arthur, "people like them should not be allowed to have children."

They all went back inside, and Frenchie had just collected his bits and pieces, when Quentin arrived back. He got out of the taxi and swept into the gallery.

"Pay the driver uncle," he called out, "I didn't have enough left, it's a disgrace how the price of gold leaf has shot up" Teddy and Arthur said good bye to Frenchie, paid off the taxi, and went into the workshop to show Quentin what Teddy had bought from Frenchie.

"Oh well done," said Quentin.

"The white creamery jug is for your Auntie Queenie," said Teddy, "perhaps you could wash it and give it to her later."

"You dear sweet thing," said Quentin, "is the romance still there even though you're divorced?"

"No it is not still there," said Teddy crossly, "its just that she collects It." And he stomped out followed by Arthur.

"Quentin locked the door behind them and got down to business. He carefully washed and catalogued the pieces Teddy had just bought. All nice pieces Uncle Teddy, thought Quentin, he certainly knew his business, he had learned most of it from his father.

He wrapped the little jug in white and gold tissue paper and placed it in one of the Galleries gift boxes. He tied a gold satin bow around the box and humming a little tune to himself he popped next door to deliver it to his aunt.

. . . .

Beth lay on the floor, in the room her parents had recently rented. There was only one bed in the room and her parents occupied that. Soon they would be back from the pub, drunk and falling about laughing. Then they would get on the bed, rolling about making lots of noise, doing things that adults do, that she didn't understand. They always told her to keep her eyes shut and she did. All she had was this old blanket to sleep on. She also had a smelly old cushion. This was her life. She would always wait until they fell into a drunken sleep and then drag herself to the toilet and back. In this room the toilet and hand basin was in the cupboard, not down the corridor as it was in some of the places they had stayed in.

Presently she heard them coming up the stairs, laughing and joking. Johnny threw a pork pie and a bag of crisps at her. She fell on the pork pie, eating it as quickly as she could, but her mouth was dry and she found it hard to swallow. She only ate if they brought her something back from the pub, and she hadn't eaten for two days.

"The girl did good," said Johnny, "got thirty quid today."

"Yer," said Fanny, and she fished in her pockets and brought out some clothes she had stolen from a second stall in the market, and threw them at Beth.

"See what you get when you earn us good money," she said, and then she and Johnny jumped on the bed for their usual afternoon romp, but as they were very drunk, they were soon asleep.

Beth dragged herself to the toilet. She tried to wash herself with toilet paper and cold water from the basin. There was no soap, hot water or flannel, only a grubby towel. She drank some water from the basin. They never ever thought that she might be thirsty. She looked at the clothes, there was a pair of clean knickers, which she really needed, a vest, a dress that was a bit large for her, but at least it was clean. There was also a pretty pink cardigan with flowers on it, but she knew she would never be allowed to wear that outside, because she had to look poor and uncared for so people would give money. Once she was dressed in her new clothes she dragged herself back to her blanket

She had saved her bag of crisps and was now going to enjoy them. She thought of the morning. Three men had put a lot of money in the hat, and one of them bought her an ice cream, something that she had never had before. It was cold, sweet, and delicious. During the latter part of the morning, someone wearing a long black cloak and hood; had whispered to her that an angel was to come and take her away to heaven. She could not see the face of this person, as the hood hung forward and covered it. She hoped the angel would come soon as the mornings were getting cold and soon she knew it would be cold all day and she would freeze. They never allowed her socks or shoes to keep her feet warm. It looked better for her to be bare footed and ragged. It brought in more money. Soon Beth fell asleep and dreamed of angels.

Chapter Five
Home Again

Detective Sergeant Boyd was waiting at Heathrow for his boss to land. Detective Chief Inspector Robert Bland, and his new wife Jean, had just spent a month in America and the Caribbean Islands. They had been married in America, this was the second time around for both of them, and Boyd was glad to see them back

Roberts first wife had died of cancer some ten years ago, and he had met Jean when he and Boyd had gone to Haversham over seven years ago to investigate three missing people from the same street, one of them being Jeans abusive husband. None of the missing were ever traced, but Robert Bland thought he knew where they were.

Seven years later he met her again, after her husband and the others had been pronounced legally dead. He and Boyd had gone back to look for a mass murderer, who they thought was hiding out in the town; and Robert decided that Jean was the woman for him, and fortunately Jean felt the same way. Now they were back to start a new life together.

Boyd breathed a sigh of relief when he saw them coming out, and pushed forward through the crowd to help them with their luggage. They had a large trolley full of luggage, and Robert was struggling to hang on to the top cases that seemed to be slipping off.

"Welcome back Sir," he said, grabbing two of the lighter cases off the top of the pile, did you have a good flight back?"

"Yes thank-you Boyd," said Bland, "I take it that it's not a coincidence that you are here."

"Not really Sir, although I would have come anyway. The Super sent me; he's been like a bear with a sore head ever since you left. I've got to tell you Sir it seems a lot longer than a month."

"Well Boyd, we have to tell you that it was not long enough for us. We nearly stayed another month, didn't we Jean?" Jean laughed as she saw the look of horror on Boyd's face.

"Car's parked outside Sir, just follow me," he said pushing through the crowd

"Boyd we are not going back to the office, you are to drive Mrs Bland and I back to the house, as we have had a very long flight. Remember Mrs Bland has never seen the house."

"Oh you'll love it," said Boyd.

"I'm sure I will," said Jean.

"When at last they drew up outside the house, Jean could hardly believe her eyes. It was an old house in soft coloured stone, and it looked like a soft gold in the afternoon light. It had arched windows and a curved gravel drive. It looked like an old manor house. Jean fell in love with it the moment she saw it.

Robert gave her a bunch of new keys that he had had especially made for her and she rushed to the front door to let herself in. The front door was large and arched made of wood with iron straps and studs down the front, and a large fancy iron key opened it. She opened the door and gasped, it was beautiful; the floor in the large hall was covered in old wonderful tiles in bright colours and patterns.

"I'm supposed to carry you over the threshold," said Bland staggering in with two of the larger suitcases.

"Oh Robert," she said, "The house is wonderful. I know you said it was old, but I had no idea of how beautiful it was going to be."

"Sorry about the size of the keys Jean but an old house requires big iron keys. Not at all convenient, for the pocket, or the handbag."

"I don't care," said Jean, "Sergeant," she said turning her attention to Boyd, "were you told to bring Robert back to the office?"

"Yes Mrs Bland."

"Then you do just that. I'll do the unpacking, do you have a washing machine Robert?"

"Oh yes," said Bland. The kitchen is quite modern, washing machine, dryer, fridges and freezers, there's an agar but I never use it. I prefer to use the gas cooker. There's also a utility room, with airing cupboards for linen, lots of storage space and a big washer dryer for doing quilts and things. Most of the stuff I don't use."

"Right," said Jean, "take those cases upstairs to the main bedroom, and those to the kitchen. You go off to work and I'll unpack and settle in, and I'll cook a meal for eight o'clock tonight, so let me know if you are unable to get back by then."

"So you want me to go?" said Bland.

"Yes," said Jean, "the quicker the better."

"Well," said Bland," being thrown out of my own house already. You only married me to carry your bags."

"Of course dear," said Jean, "and its my house now, see you at eight o' clock and bring Amanda and Boyd back with you, and we can all dine together. Right, off you both go," and she hustled them out of the house.

Bland and Boyd got into the car and they pulled out of the drive to go to the station.

"Well that's a relief," said Bland.

"What is?" said Boyd

"She likes the house."

"Anyone would," said Boyd, "Amanda loves it."

"Really," said Bland, "well then you both better make sure you turn up tonight. Jean loves making dinner for her friends."

"We'll be there with bells on," said Boyd, "should we bring some wine?"

"Don't worry I'm sure Jean will have everything sorted."

"Then we'll bring some flowers," said Boyd, "Amanda always says that you can't have too many flowers."

"I think that's to encourage you to buy her a bunch in the first place"

"Really Sir,"

"Yes really," said Bland, "But it's a nice thought Boyd, Jean really loves flowers. She will be delighted".

"Don't know what the Super is going to say Sir. He was expecting you an hour ago"

"Don't worry Boyd, I'll talk him down."

"You always do Sir."

Chapter Six
Cometh the Messenger

Beth lay on her blanket, she had been crying. He father had dropped her, as he often did, and she had grazed her arm and it was stinging. They were asleep, and today, they had brought nothing back from the pub for her, and she was hungry. She picked up yesterdays crisp bag and licked it, but she had licked all the crumbs and salt out of it yesterday.

The door to the room started to open slowly and silently. She was scared and put her hands over her mouth to stop herself crying out in fear. The hooded figure of the messenger came quietly into the room. He put his finger up to his lips to indicate that she should be quiet. She was pleased to see him. He had a pale yellow, fluffy blanket with him, which he wrapped around Beth He then gathered her up very gently, and left the room. He closed the door behind him as quietly as possible in order not to waken her parents, who were snoring away, lost to the world.

There was a black limousine with darkened windows in the street outside. He placed her in the back seat and put the seat belt across her.

"That's to stop you falling off the seat when the car is moving," he said softly, as she had looked concerned when he strapped her in.

"Are you the angel?" she asked.

"Oh no not me, I am just the messenger." He climbed into the front seat and the car pulled away.

About fifteen minutes later they pulled into the courtyard at the back of a tall house. The Messenger got out and opened the garage doors; he then drove the car into the garage and locked the doors behind them.

He carried Beth up two flights of stairs and they came into a lovely sitting room. He sat her in a big soft armchair next to the fireplace, where a fire was burning brightly in the hearth. It had been a little chill today and he thought she might feel the cold.

"Today," he said, "the Angel will come for you, but first you must have a bath and put on some clean clothes, you can't meet an Angel dressed in rags."

There was a small bath full of warm suds in front of the warm fire. He told her to take off her dirty clothes, and wrap herself in the towel, and then to call him and he would come in and lift her into the bath, he then left the room.

When she was ready she called him, and he came in and lifted her into the bath, holding the towel as she slipped into the water.

"Is that alright?" he said.

"Yes," she answered, "it's so warm and smells so nice." The Messenger washed and combed her hair for her.

"Call me when you need me," he said and then he left the room, so that she could wash herself.

She enjoyed her bath, never before had she had a soft flannel, and such beautiful smelling soap. When she was ready she called him and he brought in a warmed, large, white fluffy towel and lifted her out of the bath and on to a low stool.

"There you are," he said, "get yourself nice and dry and put on your new clothes in the order I have laid them out for you." He then cleared away the bath, and left the room.

She put on the clothes as he had told her. She enjoyed the soft feel of the underwear, and the frilly petticoat. She had never had a petticoat before. She put on the dress, but could not reach the buttons at the back, so she called the Messenger. He fastened the buttons, and tied the wide satin sash around her waist, then brushed her hair and tied it with pink ribbons, the same colour as the dress. He put clean white socks on her small feet and soft little white shoes. He lifted her up so that she could see herself in the mirror.

She gasped in surprise; she was pretty, she was not dirty and horrible, as she looked in the cracked mirror at home.

"I think we have time for tea before the Angel comes," he said, and sat her at the table. She tried everything on the table, bread and butter, honey, jams, little cakes, jelly and cream and lots of different sandwiches, even ice cream in a little glass bowl with a silver spoon. The Messenger sat watching her and suddenly said,

"Do you have any toys that you could take with you?"

"No," she said, "I have no toys." The Messenger left the room and came back with a small teddy bear and a small doll, together with a crystal necklace and a matching bracelet. He put on the necklace and the bracelet on for her, and she hugged the teddy and doll.

"I will always have these wont I," she said.

"You will have them forever," he replied. She shivered and the Messenger helped her get into a cardigan. It was pretty with flowers and ribbons on it.

"Am I beautiful, she asked.

"You are beautiful now, and you will always be beautiful," said the Messenger.

"I am very tired," said Beth, "will the Angel come soon?"

"Finish your drink," said the Messenger and Beth swallowed down the last of her milk.

The Messenger picked her up and laid her on the couch.

"Now," he said, "rest your head on this silk pillow, and have a little sleep, and when you open your eyes, the Angel will be with you and you will be in heaven."

"Is this place heaven?" she asked as her eyes fluttered.

"No," said the Messenger, "heaven is much nicer, this place can be hell," but Beth did not hear him, soon she would be dead, as the poison flowed through her body bringing her everlasting sleep.

Chapter Seven
Giles

Giles Jones sat on a bench watching the Thames flow by. Below him were steps leading down to the water. This had once been a very busy wharf area, but that time was long gone. The warehouse buildings behind him were now very expensive trendy flats, boutique shops, and eating- houses for the City people with their big fat bonuses.

There was a lot of traffic up and down the river at this time of night Boats full of revellers were going past, lights blazing and music blaring. It had just got dark and Giles was wondering what to do next. He did not want to go back to his lodgings, as he owed his landlady money and he felt that she was one step away from giving him the bum's rush. It would be better go back when she was safely tucked up in bed. He had been a good newspaperman in the old days, investigative reporting they used to call it. He had been the best, but the drink had got to him and he went downhill fast, until no one would employ him. He had pulled himself together with the help of Alcoholics Anonymous, and it had been two years since he had had a drink, but no one had given him a commission for ages.

He had his camera on the seat beside him; just one good picture would help him get on his feet again.

He thought he heard something splash into the water upstream from him. He looked around but he could not see anything. He decided he must have been hallucinating, because he hadn't eaten much during the day, but then he became aware of a light in the water bobbing towards him. He slung camera bag over his shoulder and descended down the steps. He picked up a long pole with a hook on the end, from the paraphernalia of ropes, bits of timber, and boating junk that was piled up against the wall, and waited.

As it got nearer he saw that it had two lanterns on it, the old fashioned sort, lit with candles. It looked like a very small boat, he heard a tinkling sound and could see a bell on a rod attached to the side of the boat. He reached out with the pole and drew it towards him until it bobbed against the steps the bell ringing louder.

"Christ Almighty," he said out loud, "it's a child's coffin," and in the soft glow of the lanterns he could see it had an occupant.

At first he was horrified and then his journalistic streak kicked in. He held the pole on the bottom step with his foot, to keep the coffin steady and got out his camera and started taking pictures.

The occupant was a little girl resting on a silk white pillow. She was covered in a white silk eiderdown, embroidered with masses of small brightly coloured flowers.

Tucked in her arms were a teddy and a dolly. All around the lace trimmed edge of the coffin were fresh sweet smelling flowers. There was a white card with a black trimmed border, tucked under one of her hands, which said,

> Lonely crippled child named Beth
> Who lived in misery and strife
> She had a beauty in her death
> That she had never had in life

And it was signed, **The Messenger of Death**

If he was quick enough, he would catch the press and be on the front page in the morning. He put his camera away and looked around. Two people were walking towards him. He called out to them and they came running . It was a young man and his girlfriend

The man arrived first; high spindly heels hampered his girlfriend, they were not the sort of shoe you run in.

"Quick," shouted Giles, "don't let the coffin float away, I'm going to get help." The young man took the pole, and went further down the steps until he could grab the coffin.

"For fuck's sake," he said, by now his girlfriend had arrived. When she saw the coffin and the child she started to scream. At this moment Giles made his escape. He phoned the police, as he ran to get a taxi, to go straight to the man he knew would publish the pictures – no questions asked.

The Messenger also took his leave, he had to make sure that Beth was found. Finding a man sitting there was a stroke of luck. He did not want her washed out to sea. The world would know of this child's life and death and that was just. He slipped out of the shadows where he had been hiding, and joined the throng that had gathered.

Chapter Eight
Bland and Boyd meet the Parents

Jean had prepared a really sumptuous dinner, which was enjoyed by all. Now they were sitting around having coffee and brandy and chatting. The phone went and Bland answered it. They heard him say,

"Yes Sir."

"He's here Sir."

"We'll need a driver Sir we've had a drink."

"We are off duty Sir - and can we have a camera man – Thank-you Sir."

"Yes Sir, right away Sir," and he put the phone down.

"Sorry Jean," he said, "got to go out. They have found a little girl floating down the river in a coffin."

"Oh God," said Jean, "is she dead?"

"We believe so," said Bland, "come on Boyd, you too, the car will be here in a minute, I know I've had a drink but why do I feel so tired?"

"Jet lag Sir," said Boyd. The front door bell went. It was the old sort where you pulled the handle from outside and the bell rang in the house.

"Time to go Sir."

"Don't wait up Jean," said Bland kissing the top of Jean's head.

"Sorry Amanda," said Boyd.

"Stay the night Amanda," said Jean, "then we can have breakfast together."

Bland and Boyd were driven to headquarters, and briefed by the Super.

"You go and see the body Robert, and then go and see the parents, and bring them down to identify the body."

"Do we know who they are Sir?"

"Yes we do Robert, the Messenger was obliging enough to put the parents name and address on the back of the card."

Bland and Boyd went to see the child and were shocked to see a starved, crippled waif.

"God Sir," said Boyd, "she looks as though she is a Biafran." Bland put the sheet back covering her face and they moved on to the belongings. They looked at her clothes and the toys and the coffin, and they read the card.

"Looks like someone was trying to make up for her life" said Boyd, fingering the crystal beads "and decided that she would be better off dead."

"Indeed they did," said Bland, "its murder of the worst kind. The murderer is mentally deranged; he or she thinks they are doing good, helping a soul to peace, away from their dreadful life. They are the hardest to spot because they never let their guard down."

"What now Sir?"

" Now Sergeant we have the unpleasant duty to tell the parents that their little girl has been murdered. I have a bad feeling about this Boyd. Surely they must have noticed that she is missing by now, and yet they haven't reported it."

"Well Sir, looking at the child I don't think they can be very good parents, after all the murderer wasn't responsible for her condition."

"True Boyd, very true." They went back to the car and found Max Reiner was waiting for them, to Bland's way of thinking he was the best photographer in the business

When they arrived at the address is was a run down old tenement building, there were windows missing and piles of rubbish outside.

"Well no news there," said Bland looking out of the car window, "It's what I expected."

"Blimey," said Reiner, "have we gone through a time warp and come out in Dickensian London, I didn't know streets like this still existed."

"Oh they exist," said Bland, "as do those who live in them. Come along let's get this over and done with."

They made their way up to the first floor and knocked on the door. They waited a while and there was no answer. Boyd banged on the door and they heard someone stirring. The door opened a few inches and Johnny Oates peered out.

"I'm Detective Chief Inspector Bland," said Bland showing his credentials, "and this is Sergeant Boyd and Police Officer Reiner, am I addressing Mr Oates?"

"Yer, what of it?" said Johnny, as he scratched his stomach and yawned.

"Who is it?" shouted Fanny from the bed, "tell them to bugger off."

Bland ignored the remark and continued, "may we come in Sir we have some rather bad news." Johnny pushed back the door and let them in. He stood there in his filthy underwear, and scratched himself all over giving special attention to his private parts.

Fanny sat up and said,

"What the hell did you let them in for, what do they want?"

"Shut your face woman, or I'll shut it for you," said Johnny in a menacing tone, "it's the police." Strange thought Bland, they haven't noticed Beth's absence. This is going to be difficult. Boyd was choking down the feeling of nausea. The place had the stench of unwashed bodies and dirty bedclothes, and he could smell the filthy toilet. Where did the child sleep, he thought, and then he caught sight of the foul blanket and cushion on the floor. He thought of the frail little child lying dead on the slab, back at the morgue, and he wanted to run screaming from the room. He was aware that Bland was speaking.

"Mr Oates," said Bland, "can you tell us where your daughter is?" Johnny took a look at the blanket and realised Beth was gone.

"'Ere Fanny the kids gone." Fanny sprang out of bed, and the three policemen swiftly turned their backs, while she pulled on her clothes.

"That little bleeder," she fumed, "I'll 'ave 'er guts for garters, I warned 'er what would 'appen if she tried to leave."

"And what would happen Mrs Oats," said Bland, his eyes narrowing with anger.

"I'd break 'er uver leg, I'd teach 'er to sneak off, I'd kill 'er so I would."

"Well Mrs Oates," said Bland, "you wont have to kill her because someone else has already done it for you."

There was a silence in the room as the Oates realised that they had lost their meal ticket. Not the way I should have told them; thought Bland, and then he thought, sod it – it was better than hitting Oates which is what he wanted to do. He then asked them to come and identify the body.

"I suggest you put some trousers on Sir," he said to Oates. Oates put on his jeans and tee shirt; but said nothing; neither did Fanny. They both knew nothing good was going to come out of this. They had never sent her to school, and they had managed to keep out of the way of the police and social services. What were they going to do now – no Beth – no income.

Bland said quietly to Max,

"When we are gone, photograph everything I'll get forensic up here."

"If you can promise me that I wont open a cupboard and find Fagin, you've certainly got Bill Sykes and Nancy. It's God awful Robert."

"Never mind Max, do what you do best." He turned to the Oates and said,

"We have a car waiting outside, I know it's a painful duty, but it has to be done, because we need to be sure that it is her."

They went to see the body and confirmed that it was Beth. Then they were taken to see her effects. They looked at the coffin, and the clothes and toys. Johnny slipped the beads in his pocket, and put the clothes and toys in the coffin, then he picked it up and started towards the door.

"Excuse me Sir, " said Bland, "where are you going?"

"We've done what you wanted, we've identified the body, now we are going 'ome, we might get a few bob for these bits."

"I'm sorry Sir," said the big burly policeman on the door, taking the coffin and its contents away from Johnny, "I don't think you fully understand Sir. These items are evidence and cannot be removed," he said, holding out his large hand for the crystals that Johnny had pocketed. Johnny reluctantly handed them back, "it all helps us with the enquiries into the child's death."

"When do we get them then?" said Johnny.

"You don't," said the policeman and disappeared through the swing doors.

"Well Sir this way," said Bland, "we have to have a statement and then someone will run you home."

"What for," said Johnny.

"Well Sir, we need to know when you last saw you daughter, who you think might be responsible for her abduction and death, you do want to catch her killer don't you."

"Yer, course we do don't we Fanny?"

"Course," said Fanny, although she did not sound sure.

They were taken to the interview room and given tea. They were asked when they last saw her and they said, when they came back from the pub. They were all together at three o'clock. Why had they not seen anyone come into the room and take her away? They must have been asleep. Had they been drinking? Yes, but they were not drunk, only a little merry. Why wasn't she at school? She was too ill to go to school. The questions went on, but little progress was made. They were at last allowed to go home.

Bland and Boyd went home too. It had been a long day, especially for Bland as he had come straight to work after an overnight flight. There was nothing they could do until they had the post mortem report tomorrow, and then they would bring in the parents again, for further questioning.

Chapter Nine
Giles Visits Fanny and Johnny and the Grandmother

The following day was full of the news of a child being found, in the river, but only the tabloid that Giles had sold his story to had pictures and a description of how the coffin with its lights and bell, and bobbed down the river finishing up at the wharf.

Giles was up early that morning, and thousands of pounds richer for his exclusive, he was off to follow up with interviewing the parents Johnny and Fanny Oates.

He was at their door by seven o' clock in the morning. At first Johnny Oates told him to sod off, but when Giles mentioned how much the paper was willing to pay for an exclusive story Johnny let him in. For money they were only too willing to talk and let Giles take pictures, especially for big money.

Even though Giles was a hardened newspaperman, he flinched at the squalor they were living in, and when he saw the blanket at the foot of the bed where the child was supposed to sleep, he felt anger rising inside him. A dog would have been better treated. Small wonder someone had killed the child, probably to put her out of her misery. He knew when he got back to the office with this material; his editor was going to lambaste the parents and the Social Services in tomorrows issue for allowing this to happen.

The Oates signed a contract for their exclusive story, and was going to receive a handsome amount in exchange. An amount that would take care of their pub needs for many years ahead.

"Now remember," said Giles, "you don't talk to any other newspaper or you will not get the money."

"Don't worry," said Johnny, "we know when to keep our traps shut." As Giles was leaving he asked where her toys were as it would make a nice picture featuring a doll or a favourite teddy.

"She didn't 'ave no toys," said Johnny, " couldn't afford 'em, anyway we was always on the move, no point in 'aving belongings.

"No toys!" said Giles, God these people really were the pits. His editor was going to have a field day.

"Well good-bye," he said and hurried out of the room and down the steps into the fresh air. He was wise enough to get their entire story, as he had the feeling that the police would soon be locking them up.

"When he got back to the office, the editor was over the moon with the pictures he brought back.

"Always said you were the best in the business," he said, "before you became a lush."

"Not any more," said Giles, "I've been dry for two years now."

"What ever," said the editor, but he was not really listening to Giles.

"Well Giles, as long as you can bring back stuff like this you have a place here. Tell you what, one more really good article with pictures, and you can have a permanent position on this newspaper.

"Thanks," said Giles, smiling to himself, one more article with pictures on this case and he could name his own price on any of the big newspaper.

"Don't think we'll get much more out of the Oates," said Giles, "I believe that they will be charged with cruelty and gross neglect any moment now, so we are one step ahead of the competition. What I thought of is going to see the grandparents."

34

"I thought his parents were dead?"

"So they are, but Fanny's parents are still alive. Her father won't be any use, because he is in a home in an advanced state of Alzheimer's disease, but the mother lives in the Borough High Street over a tobacconist, and she hasn't lost her marbles."

"Well get down there Giles, before the others find her, pay want you think the story is worth, and get photos, lots of photos, that's what the public want."

When Bland and Boyd arrived at the office that morning Beth's autopsy was waiting on his desk. It stated that Beth had been poisoned, but there would have been no pain, just a gradual slowing down until the heart stopped. It would have been like falling into a deep sleep. The rest was not good reading. She was underweight and undernourished and showed many instances of broken bones all over her body. Her arms, legs, several fingers, three ribs and once she had received a slight fracture of the skull. These were all old wounds and had nothing to do with her abduction and subsequent death. It was clear that she had been starved over a long period of time, probably since birth. This was why she was undeveloped for her age, and she had brittle bones, which might account for the number of breaks she had had during her lifetime. If she had not died when she did, she would have surely died during the coming winter, as she did not have the stamina to continue, any small illness would have resulted in death.

Cruelty and gross neglect by her parents should be noted and the Social Services should be informed.

Bland went down the corridor to see the superintendent and they discussed what the next move should be.

"Get the Social Services in Robert, and bring in the parents I think there is a case to answer. I'd personally like to lock them up and throw away the key, however it's not up to me. Get them in Robert and do what you have to do."

Giles left the office and made his way to London Bridge and walked slowly down the Borough High Street looking for the tobacconist .He found it and next door was a green painted front door which was the entrance to the flat above. He rang the bell and waited. There was no answer. He rang the bell again and a voice behind him said,

"You looking for Mrs Mercer?" he turned to see a young boy standing there.

"Yes son, do you know where she is?"

"She's 'aving coffee at the Pop In Parlour down the street."

"Thanks son," said Giles, and he gave the boy a tip.

"Cor a fiver," said the boy, "thanks Guv'nor," and he ran off.

Giles made his way down the street to the Pop In Parlour in time to see them all coming out.

"Mrs Mercer?" he asked one lady, and she shook her head and pointed to a small fragile lady in a blue coat. He waited for her to come level with him and said,

"Mrs Mercer?"

"Yes," she said, "what of it?"

"I'm sorry to disturb you but my name is Giles Jones and I'm from the press," and he showed her his card.

"So what," she said.

"I wonder if you would allow me to interview you about your daughter and son-in-law and your granddaughter Beth?"

"What's in it for me?"

"We would pay," said Giles, "in fact for an exclusive story just for our newspaper alone, we would pay very well indeed, especially if there were photos."

"Better come back to my house then," she said and looking at his camera bag she said,

"No pictures of me though."

"Very well," said Giles. They went back to the flat and she asked him to take a seat while she removed her coat and hat and looked out a box of old photos and bits.

"Ere," she said you can 'ave these for a fiver a piece. I don't want them, ain't no use to me now. This is Fanny and 'im, on their wedding day. Never could stand 'im. These two are of Fanny when she was small. She was a lovely baby. We only 'ad Fanny, she was our only child, but when she married that good for nuthin Johnny Oates we 'ad nuthin more to do with 'er."

As far as Giles was concerned these pictures were pure gold. His editor would jump for joy.

"Oh 'ere," she said, handing a faded print to Giles "this is one of Beth, taken soon after she was born. You can't see her gammy leg there, but she was always fragile even then." Poor little bitch thought Giles, it's a wonder she lasted as long as she did.

"Are there no other pictures of Beth?" asked Giles.

Nah," she said, "they never took any, all she was to them was a meal ticket. I knew what they were doing – begging and such. They moved all over keepin' out of the way of the authorities. " 'e claims to 'ave a bad back, bad back my arse, you should 'ave seen 'im in the street fights he got into, nobody ever got the better of Johnny Oats. Eventually they moved back 'ere. I reported them to the Social a couple of times, when I found out where they were, but they had always gone by the time the Social got there. Two weeks ago I saw the baby in the street and decided to kidnap 'ere and bring 'er 'ome 'ere wiv me. But just as I was bending over to pick 'er up, Johnny Oates sprang out of nowhere, and told me to clear off and not to come back. I'm glad she is dead and out of 'er misery. I know Fanny is my daughter but I 'ope they'll be made to pay for what they done to 'er, the bleeders."

"Can I take these?" asked Giles

" 'elp yourself, I ain't got no use for them." Giles told her what the paper was willing to pay for the interview and photos and she gasped.

"Thank-you," she said, "now I can bury my granddaughter in style and still have a fair amount to make life a bit more comfortable." Giles collected the photos and said,

"Would you mind if I bought a doll and a teddy bear to go in her coffin?"

"Course not son, it's a very kind thought."

"Good I'll drop them off later today – Mrs Mercer, my paper is not going to be kind to your daughter and son-in-law, in fact just the opposite, and I think the police will be after them as well."

Bloody good job too!" she said, "Did you take that picture of Beth in the paper, the one in the coffin?"

"I did Mrs Mercer but nobody must know because I could get into trouble."

"It was a lovely picture, she looked so beautiful with all the flowers and all. I cut it out to keep."

""Tell you what," said Giles, "when I come back with the toys I'll bring you a proper photograph. Well I must go, remember don't talk to other newspapermen or my boss will not pay up."

Mum's the word," she said and showed him out. Giles was as good as his word, later he came back with the toys, and several pictures of Beth for her grandmother.

Chapter Ten
Social Services

Bland left the Super's office and went back to his own, to find Boyd talking to three Social Service officers. He had arranged for them to have a report of Beth's condition at the time of death.

Abigail Merchant was the senior officer and she had two new people to the service with her. She jumped up when she saw Bland.

"Oh Robert," she said, "This is truly terrible."

"I know Abigail," said Bland, "how come your people never picked up on the situation?"

"We never could catch up with them. They moved all over the country and we had no idea where they were. When they moved back here, twice they were reported to us, and by the time we got there they were gone. If only more people would come forward when they know that a child is being abused, we are very discreet. The papers are going to have a field day with this Robert, and I can't say I blame them."

"We are bringing them in for questioning, would you like to sit in?" asked Bland.

"Is that wise Sir?" said Boyd.

"I can't see why not Boyd, we can get the Oates permission. Let's make it an informal meeting to start off with and see where we go from there. Beth has to be buried and arrangements have to be made so they should have no objections to the Social Services being present."

"Half an hour later they were all seated in a meeting room, except the two young social workers who had gone back to their office, leaving only Abigail, she was pleased about that because she had a yen for Bland, and would make sure that she sat next to him. The fact that he had just got married meant nothing to her. Bland asked the Oates if they minded Miss Merchant the social worker being present, as arrangements had to be made for Beth's burial. They said they didn't object.

"Won't do no good," said Oates, "we can't afford to bury 'er. The social will 'ave to do it. She was found in a coffin, bury 'er in that" Abigail could not believe her ears, and scribbled furiously on her pad.

Mr Oates," said Bland, "have you any idea why your daughter was abducted?"

"No," he said sullenly.

"Mrs Oates?"

"No," she said equally sullenly. They had just got the down payment on their interview and it was burning a hole in their pockets, they wanted to get out and start spending it.

"Mr Oates," said Boyd, "can you tell us why she was half starved?"

"No," said Oates, "it wasn't our fault.

"Mrs Oates?"

"She wasn't a big eater," said Fanny."

"Perhaps you didn't feed her," said Boyd angrily.

"That's a filthy lie," shouted Oates

"She got fed when we 'ad money," said Fanny.

"And when was that Mrs Oates?" said Bland. Fanny did not want to say that they begged: or rather Beth begged.

"When we can," she said, "Johnny 'as a bad back and can't work."

"What do you do for money?" said Bland, "are you signed on at the local office?"

"No," said Oates quickly, "not at this local office."

"Where then?" said Bland.

"If you tell us where," said Abigail, "we can have your paperwork transferred."

"We signed off where we used to be so don't get nuffin now." Strange thought Abigail, we have never been able to trace him collecting money anywhere – nor her. The truth was they were collecting payments from several different places, under false names and addresses.

"Mr Oates," said Boyd, "how do you account for the fact that your daughter suffered so many broken bones?"

"Wasn't our fault," said Fanny, "Beth couldn't walk and 'ad to be carried everywhere, and what wiv Johnny's bad back, sometimes he accidentally dropped 'er."

"Did you take her to the hospital on these occasions?"

"Nah," said Oates, "can't be doing wiv doctors and 'ospitals. I used to fix it meself by tying a stick on her arm, or leg until it was better."

"How did you know it was better," asked Bland.

"Oh you get to know after a while," said Oates.

"Yer," said Fanny, "Johnny looked after 'er good."

Bland suddenly stood up.

"Mr and Mrs Oates we are terminating this meeting. The Sergeant is going to take you downstairs where you will be read your rights, and formally charged with gross neglect, systematic starvation over a long period of time, and cruelty to a minor, causing her bodily harm and endangering her life. Do you understand?" there was a silence.

"Your will be held in custody pending further enquiries into the life and death of Bethany Francis Oates. Please take them away Sergeant." Boyd ushered them out of the room. Oates was protesting his innocence and said he would have the law on them.

" We are the law," said Bland coldly as he watched them go.

Bland left the room in a hurry, closely followed by Abigail.

"I have a feeling that we will find that there will also be a charge for fraud, they have been getting money from somewhere, you can put money on the fact that it wont be in their names, and they have been collecting from more than one office."

"That will have to be looked into," said Abigail, "I'll inform the right departments and get the wheels in motion."

They came into reception and the Desk Sergeant called Bland over.

"There are two people waiting to see you Sir, Mrs Mercer and Mr Jones." Mrs Mercer got up and came over to Bland

"Chief Inspector, I have come to claim my granddaughter's body. She has to be properly buried. Those creatures wont do it."

"I believe there will be some paperwork to be done Mrs Mercer," said Bland, "I think the parents have to sign a release form." He looked across at reception and said,

"Sergeant get Police Officer Kimble up here, " turning to Mrs Mercer he said, "Now Mrs Mercer, Officer Kimble knows all about these things. She will help you with all the paperwork and arrangements. I'm afraid I'm not up on all the facts."

Officer Kimble came in and took over. She took Mrs Mercer down to her office for a chat, and a cup of tea. As she was leaving, Mrs Mercer turned to Giles and said,

"Thank-you for walking down with me Mr Jones, and thank-you for you know what," and patted her handbag.

"Your welcome," said Giles.

"Well Giles," said Bland, "what can I do for you, I suppose that was your work in the papers?"

"Don't know what you mean Robert," said Giles, "I've just popped in to make you aware of a couple of things, strictly off the record. Tomorrow the paper is going to go for the jugular. The begging, sticking her on a blanket showing her withered leg. Making her beg to pay for their drinking habits. According to the landlord of The Bear, she only ate if they remembered to take her something home from the pub, usually pork pies and crisps. She had no toys, and apart from the rages she stood up in no clothes. She never had any socks or shoes, and slept on that filthy blanket on the floor. Several people wrote in to tell us that they had seen the parents collecting money from different offices. I've written down the office addresses here for your people," and he handed a slip of paper to Boyd, "The grandmother Mrs Mercer reported them a couple of time but they were never caught. I hope Robert that you throw the book at them," and then he got up and left the station without another word.

"Wow," said Abigail, who had been writing everything down, "I had better get back to the office, we have a lot of work to do. The office will be besieged tomorrow with people needing answers."

Chapter Eleven
Enter Louis – Exit Louis

Teddy and Arthur had been down to the lock-ups and brought back two Persian carpets. They had been in store for a few years, and Teddy thought they were in need of freshening up. He had asked their friend Omar to come down and have a look at them. Omar's father had a huge shop in the west end, where he only sold Persian rugs and carpets; very expensive rugs and carpets, which he sold to the very wealthy, and the well informed.

They lay them on the workshop floor and brushed soft, slightly dampened clothes across the surfaces to remove the dust.

"Why don't we just Hoover them," said Arthur, who was finding this a very laborious task.

"Nah," said Teddy, "we'll wait and see what Omar has to say, we don't want to pull the pile out do we?" Ten minutes later Omar came in around the back way, straight into the workshop. He walked straight over to the carpets, and one at a time he flicked the corner of the carpet over his foot, and counted the knots on the back. He had been known to do this in people's houses, without them being aware of it.

"Bloody good carpets Teddy," said Omar, "me Dad would give you a good price for them, especially the smaller one. I reckon he would keep that one for himself. It's very rare." He looked them over and told Teddy and Arthur what he thought each one was worth. Arthur's mouth dropped open,

"But they're old," he said, I fink they look old and tatty, right faded who would want them?"

"They are antique, and rare, and in surprisingly good condition. They are very highly prized by the people who know. They just need a little tender loving care, and airing, and my father has a man who uses something like a dry shampoo. He has a powder that he puts on the surface which he leaves on for a day or two, and when he removes it the colours seem to come to life, it removes all the dust and fluffs up the pile."

"We are opening in about ten days time," said Teddy, "do you think your dad would lend us your man?"

"Course," said Omar, "of course its best to hang them on a wall so everyone can get a good look at them. You need some proper bars. We'll see to that for you if you give me Dad first refusal on them."

"Done," said Teddy.

"Right," said Omar, "I'll go and join me Dad for breakfast, I'll give you a buzz later Teddy. I could get a few brownie points for this, I've not been in his good books lately," and he shot off.

"Instead of going all through this palaver," said Arthur, Couldn't we just take them down the launderette, they've got a couple of real big commercial machines along the back wall."

"Arfer don't be more stupid than you 'ave to be," said Teddy, "You don't put expensive Persian carpets in a washing machine. Every body knows that"

"I didn't," said Arthur truculently

"Anyway they weigh a piece, as soon as the machine started to spin it would be wrenched off the wall. Mind you I 'ad no idea that they were worth so much, I knew they were worth a fair bit but not that much."

It was seven thirty and they heard the shop door being unlocked and Quentin came in. He let up the security grills on all the doors and windows and came through into the workshop.

"Hello Teddy, hello Arthur," he said, "My, where did you get those two glorious carpets from?"

"From our stores," said Teddy, "we are going to have them freshened up and put on the walls."

"What walls?" asked Quentin.

"In the shop of course," said Teddy.

"I rather think of it as a salon or gallery," sniffed Quentin, "shop is so common. Nobody has asked me about putting carpets on the wall, it could ruin my whole design for the layout, but then I'm only the Artistic Director, who is going to ask my humble opinion. I'm going to make the morning coffee," he said and swept out of the workshop, sniffing into his large silk handkerchief."

"Fink we've put our boot in it Bruv," said Arthur.

"We 'ave that," said Teddy, "leave it to me." He went into the kitchen where Quentin was banging about making the coffee, still sniffing into his handkerchief.

"Is that the welcome chink of cracked pottery I hear," said Teddy, "heralding our most welcome cup of morning coffee?"

"There is no chipped china here," said Quentin huffily, "It's not in keeping with the establishment, but what would I know?"

"I'm glad you liked the carpets," said Teddy, "we brought them over this morning, but they have been in store a long time and we thought we'd get them looking at their best. Can't have anything but the best can we? You must tell them where you want they hung. It has to be the right place and you are after all in charge of that sort of thing. We didn't want our Artistic Director having to worry about menial things like putting up rails and cleaning.

"Well," said Quentin softening, "as long as they know that I am in charge."

"Of course," said Teddy, "who else?" At that moment Arthur pocked his head around the kitchen door.

Teddy," he said, "I think we might have trouble."

"You stay 'ere Quentin," said Teddy, and he peered around the kitchen door. He could see right through the workshop and out into the yard. There was a black sedan, with blacked out windows, silently and stealthily edging into the yard. Teddy took out his mobile phone, flipped it open and dialled. After a very short wait he said,

"'Arry? Teddy 'ere, remember Louis Gordino, the Cambora's bodyguard, well 'is car is sneaking into our back entrance. I think there's going to be trouble; we can't let 'is sort from across the river muscle in 'ere. What? You're coming right over, good." As he returned his mobile to his pocket he muttered, "Let's hope he gets 'ere before we 'ave three barrels of shit kicked out of us." Big Harry was the head of the local criminal element in this part of London, south of the river. Louis was from the north side of the river, and when his boss was assassinated, he crossed the river and was trying to muscle in.

The brothers went and stood in the doorway of the warehouse and the sedan came to a halt in front of them. Two huge Neanderthals dressed in black, jumped out of the front seats, and opened the door to allow Louis to alight from the back seat.

"Hello boys," he said in an oily voice, smiling at Teddy and Arthur. He was also dressed in black. He was squat and strong from his years of being a bodyguard

"What brings you this side of the river?" asked Teddy

"I was born 'ere, this used to be my manor."

"Really," said Arthur, "well it ain't no more, it's Big 'Arry's patch now."

"I don't think so," said Louis, his teeth gleaming as he continued to smile, "he's way up west, too big to deal with this end of town, so I've been settling meself in."

"That don't explain why you is 'ere now," said Teddy.

"Well," said Louis, "seems to me you are doing very nicely, you and yer bruvver, and that fat old ex-wife of yours, and not forgetting the cripple next door, and you wiv no insurance."

"We got insurance," said Teddy.

"But not the right sort," said Louis.

"And what's the right sort?" said Arthur

"Oh you know, fire, personal attack, breakages, robbery with violence."

"You ain't talking about protection racket, are you?" laughed Teddy, "Christ no one's into that nowadays. If you want to be a criminal go on the Internet like everyone else," and he laughed again, and so did Arthur.

"You'll laugh on the other side of your face when I've finished wiv you," snarled Louis his smile fading.

"As you 'aven't opened yet, and you wont 'ave any takings, and as your premiums 'aven't been set, I'll 'ave that carpet as a down payment. Roll it up boys." His minders moved forward but Teddy and Arthur stood their ground.

"Don't mind them," said Louis, "if you are going to be difficult I'll take both the carpets."

"You ain't 'aving one," said Teddy.

"Too right," said Arthur

From behind their backs, the minders produced two large baseball bats, and came forward tapping their palms with the tips of the bats. Suddenly they took a swipe at Teddy and Arthur, but in spite of being in their sixties Teddy and Arthur were still very nibble, and dodged out of the way. All of a sudden there was an ear splitting scream,

"Eeewaa," and Quentin shot out of the door, and jumped in front of Teddy and Arthur. He gave another blood curdling scream, jumped into the air, and kicked the first minder in the throat, he fell to his knees, dropping his bat and clutching at his throat gasping for air. Quentin spun around in a circle, leapt into the air again, and brought his clasped hands down on the other minder's neck and shoulder, and Teddy thought he heard something crack. He too dropped his bat and fell to the ground, yelling that his shoulder was broken, and rolled about in agony. Teddy and Arthur Grabbed up the bats and Teddy said,

"Now give us some fighting room you pair of scumbags." The pair on the floor were struggling to get up, but Louis drew a gun and threatened Teddy and Arthur.

"Drop those bats," he snarled. Teddy and Arthur threw the bats behind them.

"You old fools," he said, "who the hell did you think you were dealing with?"

"A stupid minder who let his boss get assassinated," shouted Arthur, "at least we saw Franco de Angelo off when he came to kill us, so as far as we are concerned you ain't nothing!"

"And so say all of us," said a voice behind Louis. He spun around and was faced with Big Harry and his cronies.

"Morning Teddy, and little Arthur," said Big Harry; because Arthur was Teddy's younger brother he had always referred to him as little Arthur.

"Morning 'Arry," said Teddy, "nice of you to drop by. Let me introduce you to Louis Patrino, he's selling insurance, or as you and I would put it, trying to muscle in on our side of the river with the protection racket. Not nice to my way of thinking, as we is all legitimate business men here, and we don't need 'is sort around 'ere giving the area a bad name."

"Well, well," said Big Harry, "I've 'eard about you. The minder who couldn't mind, 'ad to slink away to our side of the river to 'ide 'is shame.

Well let me tell you Patrino, nothing goes on this side of the river that I don't sanction, and we don't need losers bringing in their nasty 'abits."

"And who's to stop us?" said Louis, brazening it out, and aiming the gun at Big Harry. This was a big mistake as he now had his back to Teddy, Arthur and Quentin.

Teddy moved swiftly forward and grabbed Louis's ankles and with a sharp movement jerked them off of the ground. Louis crashed down on his face and the gun when off blowing out the front tyre of his car. The gun clattered to the ground and Louis became preoccupied with his broken and bleeding nose. The gun had lost its importance now, and one of Big Harry's henchmen, stepped forward and picked the gun up and slipped it into his pocket. Quentin had kicked Louis two minders in the face, and they were both out cold.

"Now," said Big Harry as he grabbed Louis by the throat, "you and me is going to 'ave a little chat at my warehouse, about who does what, and which side of the river he does it on." He snapped his fingers and two of his men moved forward and bundled Louis minders in the back of Louis car, then backed the car out of the yard with the burst tyre making a curious plopping sound as it went. Harry had Louis taken out to his car, which was parked in the street outside.

"Well Teddy," he said, "there goes the last of the rubbish, you wont be seeing 'im again. By the way me and the missus is coming down to your official opening, it looks like it's going to be a bit of a do."

"Oh yes," said Teddy, "Lots of people are coming. We 'ave got west end caterers in, and the will be plenty of champagne."

"It sounds like the bizz Teddy," said Big Harry.

"I 'ope you don't fink it a bit of a cheek, but me and Arthur were wondering, if you and you good lady would like to officially open the proceedings. You've only got to cut the ribbon, and say a few words. The press is going to be there, so it would be nice to have a local business man, such as yourself." Teddy knew that this would appeal to the man's vanity, as he so wanted to be respectable. Having his picture in the paper opening a local function would make him feel famous and important. Added to which Teddy did not want Big Harry getting ideas about starting a protection racket himself.

"Oh Teddy," said Big Harry spreading his arms out as though he was about to hug him, "me and the missus will be tickled pink. We'll see you then." And he disappeared out of the yard.

Teddy, Arthur and Quentin breathed a sigh of relief.

"Well," said Quentin, "I think we'll have that cup of coffee, we certainly deserve it."

"Quentin," said Teddy, "where did you learn to fight like that? You're a regular Kung Fu artist."

"Well Uncle Teddy, if you are different at school you get picked on and beaten up. Imagine me tall, thin, geeky looking, part Chinese and later gay, what chance did I stand? One day I was beaten up three times and I made up my mind that I was never going to be on the receiving end again, so I went to live with my Chinese grandfather and he taught me all I know."

"You're just like Bruce Lee," said Arthur admiringly.

"Oh don't," said Quentin, "you'll embarrass me," and he bustled about making the coffee.

Chapter Twelve
Another Visit from the Messenger of Death

Meanwhile in the Bland household Jean was getting ready to go to her own house in Haversham, and visit her son David. Bland was sorry that he couldn't go with her, but she insisted that he had to stay and catch the killer of the little girl, and to see that her parents got what was coming to them.

"What about David?" he said. David was Jean's son by her previous marriage

"Oh he'll understand," she said, "we can all get together when the Galleries open and you've solved the case."

"That's only ten days away," said Bland, "no pressure then."

"I have every faith in you Darling, you'll solve it in no time. Now get ready its gone nine o' clock and Darren will be here to pick you up soon." Bland looked at his watch,

"He should have been here long before now, something must have held him up." Just at that moment Boyd arrived and he looked very solemn

"Problems?" said Bland quietly.

"Tell you in the car Sir," said Boyd. Jean breezed into the hall,

"Hello Darren, you're a little late this morning,"

"Hello Mrs Bland, I got caught in the traffic."

"Well off you go Darling," she said and kissed Bland on the cheek, "I'll call you later, and I should be back in a couple of days." Bland and Boyd said their good byes and headed for the car.

"What's happened?" asked Bland

"Two deaths Sir."

"Two?"

"Yes Sir, Louis Patrino, you remember him Sir, he was minder to Michael Cambora,"

"Ah yes," said Bland, "not a very good one to let his boss get killed, and who was the other person?"

"The old tramp Willy Johnson. The Superintendent is going ballistic"

"Well deaths happen," said Bland.

"Deaths happen yes, but murders no, according to the Super."

"Oh I see," said Bland getting into the car.

"Willy was killed by the Messenger of Death," said Boyd pulling out into the traffic.

"Oh Christ," exclaimed Bland.

"Yes Sir he was found in the Travellers Rest pub. The landlord came down stairs from his flat above, at seven thirty this morning, and found him sitting in the old oak chair by the fire in the main bar. He was very clean, he'd had a bath, and his beard was trimmed, and his hair cut. He was wearing a tweed suit and looked very dapper. I've got to take you straight there."

"And Louis Patrino?"

"He was found just before I came out, that's why the Super went mad. Patrino was found underneath a railway arch, hanging upside down with his throat cut. He was still bleeding, and the doc' reckons it could only happened minutes before. A chap walking his dog found him, and he said he saw two men running away from the scene. Detective Atkins has been sent to deal with that one."

"Thank goodness for that," said Bland, "we can't follow everything up."

When they arrived at the Travellers Rest, the landlord and his wife were huddled together in a small private bar with a policeman standing by.

"Mr and Mrs White Sir," said the policeman.

"Thank-you constable," said Bland, "I believe you found him Mr White?"

"Oh yes Sir, fair gives me the creeps it does, sitting there for all the world as though he was still alive. The Missus screamed the place down, didn't you Kath?"

"It's 'orrible, orrible," she said sniffing into her handkerchief."

"Well," said Bland, "the Sergeant and I will take a look at the body meanwhile Constable I think Mr and Mrs White should be allowed to get dressed and have some breakfast, and we will talk to them a little later, when they are feeling better."

"Yes Sir," said the Constable, " the body's through there, Sir in the main bar."

"Thank-you constable," said Bland, and he and Boyd walked through into the other bar. The forensic team were there, waiting to get started.

"God," said Boyd, "I can see what Mr White meant, he looks as though he's still alive." There were flowers on the table in front of him and in his hand was a black edged card. Boyd took it and read it out loud.

Gentleman of the open Road
Never at home, never at rest
No place for him, no warm abode
Forever moving on a quest

Cruel nature dealt a tragic blow
A cancer grew within his chest
Racked in agony, full of woe
He moved towards his final rest.

> **No friends or family ties has he**
> **Alone and friendless on he goes**
> **The Messenger helped him, now he's free**
> **In death he finds a sweet repose.**
> **The Messenger of Death**

One the back of the card was written.

William James Johnson of no fixed abode
Born 26th June 1953

"What I can't understand Sir is, why was he found here?"

"The answer is in the name of the pub Boyd, 'The Travellers Rest', what could be more appropriate than that?"

"Oh yes Sir I didn't think of that. Well thought out."

"Oh yes," said Bland, peering at the body, "even his nails are clean. He's been somewhere with somebody, he didn't die quickly. Look how well his hair has been cut and his beard trimmed. These clothes are of good quality, as is his underwear," said Bland looking under his shirt, "this cravat is made of pure silk." Bland then looked under the table.

"His shoes are of good quality leather," he observed, "the Messenger obviously gave him a good farewell. He might have been with him a couple of days. I bet the pathologist will find that his last meal was a good one."

"What's the messenger all about Sir?"

"Simple," said Bland, "he's just putting people out of their misery."

"Bloody Hell," said Boyd, "then we've got no idea who is going to be next."

"You got that in one Boyd, we have no way of knowing who is going to be next."

Chapter Thirteen
William James Johnson

Three days before his death, William had bumped into an old friend. They hadn't seen each other for years, and Willy went back to his friend's house for dinner.

He was in this part of London because of his medication. He was now taking liquid morphine, as cancer had now invaded all parts of his body, and most of the time he was rigid with pain. There was nothing more that the doctors could do for him, so it was just a question of time.

His friend was visible upset to see the plight he was in, and said he must stay with him. Willy said he would stay a couple of days only, as he knew what the end would be like, and he didn't what his friend to see it. He asked his friend to help him find a room. He had a little money, at least enough to see him out. His friend said that he must stay at least three days, and then he would take him to a pub that let out rooms, it was clean and comfortable and reasonable cheap, and was quite close to Guy's Hospital where he was being treated. He would arrange everything for him.

One his first night with his friend Willy soaked in the bath and retired to a huge soft warm bed. It was heaven. The next day his friend provided him with new clothes and he took a trip to the barbers to have his hair cut and beard trimmed. He visited the hospital in the afternoon, and renewed his prescription; he now had enough to last him for a while. The doctor was pleased that he was at last under cover, and had someone to take care of him. They had been trying to get him into the local hospice, but he refused to go. After a good evening meal they played chess and talked of old times. During the night the pain became so bad that he hoped he would die, he prayed for it. His friend sat with him holding his hand, and giving him his medicine every four hours. Oddly enough he felt a lot better the next morning. They had a leisurely breakfast – full English- as they say. His friend said that he had arranged a room for him at the pub nearby, and he would take him over that night when the pub was closing, and meanwhile they would have a good day. They would visit a few old haunts, and have a good meal in the evening, before he went to the pub. He had a very good day; the pain was there, but just bearable. He didn't know that his friend had doubled the dose of medicine he was giving him.

He had all his favourite foods that night; his friend laid on a good spread. He drank wine and brandy, which usually he could not take because it burned his stomach. This evening the pain seemed to have subsided although he was beginning to feel a bit numb. His lips felt tingly but he was at that moment in time, content. A voice broke into his thoughts.

"Come along old friend, I hadn't noticed the time. The pub will be closed by now, and we shall have to go around the back." Willy got up and he and his friend went arm in arm down the road to the pub. There was no one about and it was very quiet. They were both a little worse for wear, due to the drinks they had consumed. He friend took him in through the back door and led him through into the main bar.

"Sit here old friend by the fire and rest, while I go and look for the landlord." Willie sat in a big oak chair by the fire and he leaned back, it was very comfortable. Soon his friend was back and he placed a bowl of flowers on the table in front of him. They smelled very sweet. He found that he couldn't speak now, however a feeling of peace flowed over him and at that moment he could feel no pain. His friend was putting a card in his hand. He thought perhaps it was one of those new fangled door cards but he did not care. He closed his eyes on the world for the last time and death overtook him. A tear ran down the messenger's face and as he bent forward to kiss Willy on his forehead, it dripped onto Willy's face and ran down his cheek.

"Good-bye my dear old friend," said the Messenger, "rest in peace," and he turned and left the pub.

Chapter Fourteen
Queenie's Visit

The papers were full of the death of Beth. The parents were vilified. People were turning up to testify against them. The police station and the children's' department at the council were besieged.

Bland and Boyd interviewed the White's at the Travellers Rest and went back to the station. Angry people surrounded the desk sergeant.

"Will you all please go and sit down," he looked around, "Constable," he shouted, "get everybody's name and address and then we can take statements in an orderly fashion." Bland and Boyd made a dash for their office. Once inside with the door, shut they breathed a sigh of relief.

They went through the paperwork on their desks,

"Says here Sir," says Boyd, "that they can't trace any of the clothes or items belonging to Beth, not even the coffin. The clothes were Victorian, hand sewn."

"This man is very clever," said Bland, "I'll bet a pound to a pinch of shit, that we wont be able to trace the clothes on the tramp either."

"It's going to be hard to find him Sir, if we can't pick up any clues."

"There's going to be more deaths Sergeant but hopefully He'll become over confident and less careful."

" Lets hope so Sir," said Boyd.

"Queenie had just put the finishing touches to the new stock she had just laid out, and she looked around, everything looked splendid but she thought that Quentin would probably rearrange things, she did not mind that, as he had such a good eye. She had bought an old fifties ball gown and wanted it go in the window, as her main display item, for the opening. She put on her long black coat, and switched off the radio, tut- tutting at the news that had just come through. She closed the door and locked up, and then went next door to see Quentin.

Teddy and Arthur and Quentin were having coffee and fancy biscuits, and were browsing through the new brochures that had just been delivered.

"Aven't you lot started work yet! It's half past ten," she said disapprovingly, oh is that the new brochure? Pass one over here, and yes please I will have a cup of coffee."

"Ain't backwards in coming forwards are you," said Teddy, "anyway we 'ad a bit of a set too this morning."

"Who with?" said Queenie helping herself to the biscuits."

"That prat Louis Patrino, "he came round 'ere wiv 'is hard men trying to cane us for protection money. You should 'ave seen Quentin, he's a regular Kung Fu fighter."

"What happened to him?" demanded Queenie.

"He went off wiv Big 'Arry," said Arthur.

"And now," said Queenie," white-faced, "he's just been found dead, 'anging upside down under a arch wiv 'is throat cut – I 'eard it on the news just before I came round 'ere."

"Oh Jesus Christ," exclaimed Teddy, "not 'Arry, I've just invited him to open the Galleries as a leading business man of the area. I didn't want 'im getting ideas about starting up 'is own protection racket.

"Arry didn't do it," said Arthur.

"Ow do you make that out," said Teddy.

"Simple," said Arthur, "Arry wouldn't shit in 'is own back yard."

"Oh really!" said Queenie, "don't be so uncouth Arfer."

Arthur shrugged his shoulders.

"No, Arfer's right," said Teddy, "in fact I 'eard that the mother of the Cambora's was really sore about 'er sons deaths. She put a contract out on Franco de Angelo, why not the minders who were supposed to be taking care of them."

"Seems reasonable to me," said Arthur.

"Anover thing you might not 'ave 'eard," said Queenie; "is that old tramp Willy Johnson has been killed by the Messenger of Death. They found 'im in the Travellers Rest sitting in the chair by the fire for all the world as though he was still alive and waiting for a drink"

"Bloody Hell," said Arthur, "who is going to be next?"

"Uncle Teddy," said Quentin tremulously, "they won't come after us and cut our throats will they?"

"Nah," said Teddy, "we're okay."

"I'd just die of embarrassment if I were found hanging upside down with my throat cut."

"As you would already be dead," observed Arthur, "it wouldn't matter how you we found." Quentin made a small choking sound and went into the workroom to continue work on the mirror. Queenie got up to follow him.

"Quentin dear," she said, "I've just bought a nineteen fifty's ball gown and I would love to have it displayed for the opening, it's going to be my statement piece. Can you come and have a look at it?"

"Of course Auntie," said Quentin, "I'll come along after lunch if I'm still alive, and I will do my poor best for you," and he sniffed into his large handkerchief again and sighed. As Queenie turned to go Teddy said,

"Queenie why don't you get some new clobber? You wear that long black coat all the time. It's pulled in at the waist showing your enormous bum, what wobbles as you walk, and your boobs look like those big round gas balloons waiting to take off. Can't you wear something less tight and more flowing?"

You're bloody rude," said Queenie heatedly, "no wonder I divorced you all those years ago. I've been told that I am a fine figure of a woman."

"Who told you?" laughed Teddy, "someone from St Dunstan's when he was out walking 'is guide dog?"

"That does it," she said and stormed out. Teddy and Arthur were singing under their breath as they had done many times before 'it must be jelly cos jam don't shake that way' and then they fell about laughing.

Chapter Fifteen
David and Seth

Jean arrived back at her own house and after being away for a month and she decided it was in need of a good clean. Her son David and his friend Seth did their best, but it was not up to Jean's standard.

Neither of them was a home when she arrived, so she went into a frenzy of cleaning straight away. The washing machine had not been used this much in all the time she had been away.

She put a casserole in the oven in case the boys came in later, but they didn't arrive until eight o' clock that night.

"Is that you Mum?" shouted David.

"No! Its your friendly neighbourhood burglar," shouted Jean, "who did think it was? Not many burglars switch on all the lights, and are sitting on the sofa watching television, sipping a gin and tonic."

David came in and hugged his mother.

"You look well and happy," he said, it's the happiest I have ever seen you look. I kept the secret well didn't I? I never let slip what Robert was up to, and you said yes, and went that very night. Everybody was so surprised. What was the trip like? Have you any photos of the wedding? What's Robert's house like?"

"One question at a time," laughed Jean and she turned to Seth who had followed David in and was standing quietly by while David greeted his mother.

"Hello Seth dear."

"Hello Mrs Bland."

"Seth call me Jean, well what have you two been up to?"

"The band has been offered a recording contract by one of the big company's but it would mean going to America," said David watching his mother's face.

"That's splendid," said Jean, "when do you leave?"

"In about three weeks, you know how it is, contracts to be sorted, work permits to be acquired, travel arrangements, and finding somewhere to stay at the other end. Still our manager is doing most of that."

"And you Seth," said Jean, "what about you?"

"I'm going to America next week, I have a twelve week engagement in Las Vegas, and then I'm to play a part in a film. I was really lucky. An American agent was in the club one night, and thought I'd be just right for a film that a friend of his was casting for, and he also got me the Las Vegas job."

"David," said Jean, "there is a casserole in the oven and veg in the steamer, why don't you dish us up a meal. I've been working all day and I'm pooped."

"Will do," said David, "I'll set it all up in the dining room, and then I'll give you a call," and he disappeared into the kitchen.

"Well Seth?" said Jean, her son David had recently discovered he was gay and was taking time to get used to the idea. He wasn't sure that he wanted to be gay, but as his mother said, 'let's all be what we are.' Seth on the other hand had always known that he was gay. He was a female impersonator and a very good singer, and he was in love with David, but David was completely unaware of his feelings. Seth never said anything but Jean knew, and felt sorry for him.

"Nothing to tell Jean, we are just good friends, that's all."

" Will you be close to each other when you are in America?"

"No, I'll be in Vegas and he'll be on the coast, and the film is to be shot in Paris, France.

"I'm sorry," said Jean.

"That's life," said Seth, "there is nothing to be done."

"Let's get a drink," said Jean.

"Good idea," said Seth. He poured them both a drink.

"Here's to absent friends," said Jean.

"Here's to absent lovers," said Seth, and they clinked their glasses.

"Oh very nice," said David, who had just walked in, "there's me slaving away in the kitchen getting the dinner and setting up the table, while you two are getting sozzled.

"I'm just pouring you one," said Seth.

"David," said Jean

"Yes Mum,"

"Do shut up, you only had to dish it up."

"I know," said David, "but look how elegantly I threw the knives and forks on the table." They all laughed and sat down to eat.

Chapter Sixteen
Bland and Boyd make some Visits.

The following day the Oates appeared in court for a preliminary hearing, and it was decided that there was a case to answer and the Oates were placed on remand. No bail was set; as the opinion was that they would abscond as soon as they were released, not that they could have afforded it anyway.

Beth's funeral was on Friday, and permission was given for them to attend – in handcuffs – with a larger than usual police escort.

Beth's grandmother would have preferred not to have them there at all. Bland and Boyd had to be there to make sure there were no disturbances. There would also be a few plain clothed police in the crowd, in case the crowd became unruly as feelings were running high.

Bland and Boyd walked back to the station in silence. Bland was annoyed with himself as he did not have an inkling about this case. Even though there had been two murders, and he knew there would be more, finding the killer was not going to be easy.

"Boyd," said Bland, "I think we'll visit an old friend this morning."

"Who Sir?"

"Teddy, he and his brother and Frenchie were probably the last people to see her alive. You never know what we might pick up. We're certainly doing nothing here."

"Okay Sir."

They parked in the yard at the back of the Galleries, and as they got out of the car Teddy came out of the workshop to great them.

"Allo Mr Bland, 'allo Sergeant, nice ter see yer. Come in and 'ave a cuppa."

"Thanks Teddy a cuppa would be most welcome, we've come to see how you are getting on, and to have a little word about Beth."

"Nasty business that," said Teddy, "very nasty."

"Arfer, put the coffee pot on, we 'as got guests, Mr Bland and 'is sergeant is 'ere." They trooped inside and Arthur made coffee, and got out the large tin of fancy biscuits.

"On very nice," said Bland dipping into the tin, "very nice indeed, wouldn't you say Sergeant?"

"Very tasty Sir," said Boyd also dipping into the tin.

"When you've 'ad your coffee Mr Bland we'll give you a tour of our Galleries, won't we Arfer."

"Oh yes indeed," said Arthur.

"Tell me about Beth," said Bland.

"Not much to tell really Mr. Bland," said Teddy, "Arfer saw 'er on the street corner, begging on that filthy old blanket. Me and Frenchie, who was 'ere at the time, and Arfer put some money in 'er 'at, and then that bleeder Johnny Oates appeared and 'it 'er, he took the money, and disappeared. Frenchie bought 'er an ice cream didn't he Arfer."

"Yer," said Arthur, "but she didn't 'ave that long. There was a flatfoot coming down the street and Johnny Oates appeared again, he threw the ice cream away, 'it 'er again, grabbed up Beth and 'er blanket and disappeared into the crowd."

"Anything else you can tell us about her?" said Boyd.

"No Son," said Teddy, "didn't know they were back until we saw Beth in the street."

When they had finished their coffee, and two layers of biscuits, Bland and Boyd were given the grand tour. They were very impressed with how the Galleries were coming along.

"You've got some wonderful furniture here, " said Bland, "I'll bet Jean will be interested in purchasing some pieces for the house. Steve's painting only seems to get better and better. I imagine that Jean will be spending there too. Better warn the bank. Everything is just superb, isn't it Sergeant."

"Oh yes Sir, I can't think how much Amanda will want to spend."

"You have a real talent for display Quentin," said Bland.

"Oh Chief Inspector you're too, too kind," said Quentin going all girly.

Quentin is our Artistic Director," said Teddy, "give the Inspector a brochure Quentin, Show him your picture." Quentin dashed into the office and returned with two brochures, he gave Bland and Boyd one each, and pointed out his photograph, and the article about him.

"It's a very good likeness," said Bland, Mrs Bland will be pleased to get a brochure, Thank-you Quentin."

"Yes, thanks a lot Quentin," said Boyd.

"Your welcome," said Quentin beaming.

"Teddy, that mirror that Quentin is restoring in the workshop. I think that Mrs Bland would love it, all depending on the price of course. It looks antique and expensive."

"It hasn't got a price yet Mr Bland, it depends on the outcome of the restoration," said Teddy.

"Well," said Bland, "the Sergeant and I are going to pop up and see Frenchie now, thanks for showing us around."

"We'll see you opening day," said Arthur.

"I don't think Mrs Bland would allow us not to," said Bland, We'll be there with bells on, won't we Sergeant?"

"I'll say Sir, me and Amanda will definitely be there."

"Good," said Teddy, "not long to go now and we've got a pair of really good Persian carpets coming tomorrow, they are going up on the back wall."

"Now don't forget Mr Bland, it's Saturday week," said Arthur.

"See you all then," said Bland and as they were going out of the door Quentin said,

"Don't you go buying any of that old tat, that Frenchie sells in his so called antique shop, if you want something nice you come to us," and then he scuttled back into the workshop.

Bland and Boyd turned into the main road, joining the slow moving traffic. Frenchie's place was about half a mile up on the left and it was uphill, they parked in a small car park that still had a place left, so they could walk the extra few yards to his shop on the next corner.

" Let's have lunch first," said Bland, "Look there's a pub called 'The Merchant Seaman,' let's try that." Boyd always had his doubts about Bland's choice of eating establishments. In their long association he had eaten in some very bizarre places, and this was no different. There wasn't a single customer, and it was eerie, quiet and dark.

There was a bottle blonde behind the bar, showing rather more cleavage than was good for a man's heart. She wore bright red lipstick matching the long red talons of fingernails on her hands. Her long glittery earrings resembled the hanging gardens of Babylon. The ends of which almost rested on her ample bosoms. They jangled as she walked. She was chewing gum, but pushed it to one side of her mouth to ask them if they wanted food.

" What have you?" asked Bland.

"Oh, cheese rolls, pork pies, crisps, nuts and cheese biscuits."

"Cheese rolls Boyd?" asked Bland.

"Okay Sir," said Boyd. Bland ordered two cheese rolls and two beers.

"Go and sit down," said the girl handing Bland his change, "and I'll bring it over to you. Bland and Boyd went and sat by the window, which enabled them to people watch, while they wanted for their lunch.

"Allo Mr Bland," said a voice behind them.

"Teddy," said Bland gasping and putting his hand over his heart, " you nearly gave me a heart attack creeping up like that, what are you doing here?"

"I might ask you the same thing Mr Bland."

"Lunch," said Bland.

"What 'ere?"

"Why not?" demanded Bland.

"Ain't no food 'ere," said Teddy, "least ways, none worth eating. Anyway Mr Bland just a little tip, didn't like to say anything back there, Quentin gets a bit nervous and upset. There's going to be trouble at the funeral. Better make sure that the old bill is about Sir. That's all I'm saying, see you Saturday week, " and he went as quickly as he came. The girl came across with a tray. She placed the two beers and two rolls on the table and went back to the bar still chewing her gum.

Bland bit into his roll very carefully, but it was freshly made with real butter, and strong cheddar cheese, the roll was fresh and crispy, also on the plate, was crunchy pickled onions. The beer was good too.

They had their lunch and wandered up the road to Frenchie's. An old fashioned bell jangled as they went through the door. It was like Aladdin's cave inside. The shop was stacked from floor to ceiling.

"Blimey," said Boyd, "you can't see the wood from the trees in here."

Frenchie came through from the back room,

"Inspector," he said, "what a nice surprise, to what do I owe ze pleasure of your visit?"

"It's about Beth, Frenchie, we've been to see Teddy and Arthur and it seems that you three were probably the last to see her alive, apart from her parents and the killer."

"Nothing to tell," said Frenchie, "the family moved back about three weeks before she died. I only knew because I'd seen her on street corners. Poor little child, who knows what she had suffered before 'er death. We gave her some change and I bought 'er an ice cream. Much good that did her Johnny Oates punched her in the face and threw it away, the he ran off wiz her because he saw a policeman coming."

"Flatfoot?" queried Boyd.

"Yes Boyd it's an old term for the policeman on the beat."

"Ah," said Boyd understanding at last.

"The rest you know Inspector," said Frenchie. While Frenchie was talking Bland's eyes had been scanning the goods in the shop. He had seen something when he first came into the shop that made him think of something else. Frenchie, appearing from the back room, had distracted him, and now he could not remember what it was. It would probably come to him later.

"Any idea who did it Inspector, " said Frenchie.

"No," said Bland, "but now we have two deaths and we've got to do something. Well Frenchie, we must be off, we've got work to do, Thank-you for your time. Come along Sergeant back to the office.

Chapter Seventeen
Lenny's Information

On their return to the station Bland and Boyd found a lot of reports on their desks. Bland had a message to report to the Superintendent. He went along to his office knowing he had nothing tangible to tell him.

He tapped on the door and went in.

"Afternoon Robert."

"Afternoon Sir."

"Look Robert, how is this Messenger of Death case going at the moment?"

"Not well Sir," said Bland, "they are random killings, there's no connection between, except for their situation, one dying of cancer and one dying of starvation and cruelty. There's no way of telling who is going to be next. We can't monitor everyone who is dying or has a bad life scenario. Boyd and I went to see the Hugget brothers, and Frenchie la Roche this morning, as they seem to be the last ones to have contact with her before she died, except her parents and the killer of course, but nothing new came up."

"Yes, yes, yes," said the Super impatiently, "Robert, remember that black book that was left on your desk? Before you cleared off to America You know the one that belonged to Johnny Briggs,"

"Yes Sir, I remember it well, if you remember Sir, I got shot following up information in that book."

"Be that as it may Robert, I want you to read the passages that I have put markers in. I know you have other work but I need your opinion. I gave it to Davis to read and all he said was 'very nice Sir' where do we get our recruits from nowadays. Anyway you read it and come and see me Monday morning to report."

"Yes Sir."

"Well that's all Robert, unless you have something to say."

"No Sir."

"Right off you go," he said and turned his attention to the papers on his desk. Bland went back to his office to find that Boyd had put a cup of coffee on his desk.

"Thank-you Boyd."

"You welcome Sir," said Boyd, "I thought you might need it as we haven't got any further with the case, and I thought he might have a go."

"He doesn't seem to care," said Bland, "he given me Johnny Briggs book, he's marked out passages that he wants me to read, and I have to report back on Monday, can you believe it?" He passed the book to Boyd,

"Here you read it as well. Two heads are better than one even if one is only a sheep's head."

"Baa Sir," said Boyd laughing.

"I didn't mean you Boyd and well you know it. I'm the one with the woolly sheep's head. I can't seem to go forward with this case. Not a bloody clue. You know Boyd when I was in Frenchie's shop yesterday I saw something that rang a bell, it reminded me of something else, something to do with the case. Then Frenchie came bustling in and broke my thread, and now I can't for the life of me remember what it was."

"Perhaps you ought to go back Sir."

"Perhaps," said Bland idly leaving through the papers on his desk, anything interesting in the book?"

"Well Sir, it seems to be to do with this chap called Ivan the Terrible. That can't be his real name Sir, can it?"

"Most assuredly not Boyd, Ivan the Terrible died centuries ago."

"He seems to be a nasty piece of work Sir."

"A killer?"

"Oh yes Sir, definitely a killer, but he was bizarre."

"I'll take it home and read it tonight Boyd, Jean won't be back until tomorrow." There was a silence in the office for a while as they were both reading. Bland was reading the autopsy reports again trying to see if there was something that he had missed.

The desk sergeant popped his head around the door and said,

" There's someone to see you in reception."

"Who is it?"

"He won't give a name."

"Then I won't see him," said Bland.

"He says he has some information for you, and only you, it's about the Messenger of Death."

"Oh alright I'll come and see him, tell him I'll be out in a moment Sergeant."

"Yes Sir," he said and disappeared back to his desk.

"Well Boyd you had better come with me, he's probably on the tap."

"Tap Sir?"

"Yes he's probably going to try and sell me some information. Let's go and see what he wants."

There were a lot of people milling around in the reception area. The desk sergeant indicated with his pen to a man sitting in the far corner.

"Well, well, " said Bland, "Lenny the Dip, known associate of Big Harry, he'd sell his own grandmother for sixpence." They made their way through the crowd to where Lenny was sitting.

"Allo Mr Bland," said Lenny in an obsequious manner. Oily little bastard thought Bland.

"Well Lenny what can we do for you?"

"Can we go somewhere private?" said Lenny sidling up to Bland and looking nervously around. They took him into a side office, and sat at the interview table.

"As I said before Lenny," said Bland, "what can we do for you?"

"It's more of what I can do for you Mr Bland," he said, smiling his oily smile, "I 'as valuable information that must be worth something."

"You tell us what it is and we'll decide if it's worth anything," said Bland. The smile faded from Lenny's lips.

"Got to make a living Mr. Bland," he said humbly.

"But you don't have to put the hard word on everybody," said Boyd in annoyance. Lenny ignored Boyd's outburst and continued,

"Well it's like this Sir, I was in the area the afternoon that little girl Beth was taken."

"What on earth were you doing there, it's a godforsaken hole," said Boyd.

"I was doing a bit of business in one of the flats. When I came out, this big black limo was parked outside. It 'ad black windows and you couldn't see inside, so I went across the road, out of sight in an alley, and waited. I didn't 'ave to wait too long because this really weird bloke came out, he was wearing a long monk's 'abit, with the 'ood pulled down over 'is face so you couldn't see who it was. He was carrying a child in a big yellow blanket, you could just see the top of 'er head. He put 'er in the back seat of the car and then drove off."

"Did you get the car's number?" asked Boyd.

"No, the car didn't 'ave one."

"Why didn't you come forward before?" said Bland, "why did you wait until now?"

"I know," said Boyd, "it's because he could not find the owner of the car. He was hoping to blackmail him, failing that, he's come to try his luck on us."

"Don't be like that," whined Lenny, "it must be worth something to yer." Bland slipped him something and told him to clear off, which he did – pronto. After he had gone Boyd said,

"You shouldn't have given him anything, the odious little creep."

"He speaks well of you too," muttered Bland.

"You should have made him sign a statement Sir."

"You never get statements from people like him Boyd, you know that. He's just an informant. If they had to sign a statement, information would just dry up. You get a lot of misinformation but every now and again you get a real gem."

"Not this time Sir."

"No Boyd, not this time, but it's something else we know. As I said before the abduction was well planned."

"Do you think the murderer lives in the area Sir?"

"Oh yes Boyd, how far would a car with no number plates driven by a hooded monk get, before someone got curious, or he was caught on camera? That's an idea Boyd, do a mile radius from the Oates place camera search. Garages are a good bet, because if he filled up with petrol he would not wear the monks outfit, and he might possibly have used a credit card although I think that's highly unlikely. Make it between three and six o' clock in the afternoon on that day. Also get the black book signed out. We've had a couple of late nights, so today we will go home early," he said looking at his watch, "it's six o' clock so chop, chop Boyd, let's get out of this place."

"Sir Amanda and I want to invite you to dinner tonight, the usual place, our treat."

"Are you sure Boyd?"

"Yes Sir, Mrs Bland is away and Amanda insists"

"In that case Boyd all the more reason to get a hurry on before someone finds us something else to do."

"Yes Sir," said Boyd, as they hurried through the swing doors and out of the building the desk sergeant called out to them.

"The desk sergeant is calling us," said Boyd.

"Such a pity we can't hear him," said Bland as the turned into the car park.

"Yes Sir," said Boyd as he got into the car and drove off at speed.

Chapter Eighteen
The Messenger Visits His Next Soul.

The Messenger was having his breakfast and watching the news on television at the same time. After the news there was a morning magazine programme. There was an item about Will Hargreaves, the champion cyclist who had won a gold medal at the Olympics. A lorry had hit him, while he was out on an early morning training run. That had been three months ago and now he was severely disabled. His back had been broken in several places, as was his neck. His whole body was paralysed, and he had a brace under his chin to hold his head up. He was unable to speak, neither could he eat properly, so all his food had to be pureed so that he could suck it through a small tube. This to was becoming more difficult as he did not seem to be able to digest his food properly and they had decided to put him on a drip.

Poor sod thought the Messenger, can't even take a pee. The woman on the television was saying that he had no life at all and he should be allowed to die. A man replied that it was wrong to take life. There was always hope.

"Hope! What hope?" demanded the woman, "his spine and neck can't be repaired. His body is getting weaker, he can't use his bowels, everything has to be taken away from him in a bag, someone has to do everything for him, and he can't even speak. That's not a life it's a punishment."

"Where will it all end?" said the man, "will we get rid of the old because they have become a nuisance?"

"It works in Switzerland," said the woman. The Messenger switched the television and decided that he would make a hospital visit this very morning, and see for himself.

The young man was in a specialist hospital, and it was not easy to walk about there, as there were few visitors and any stranger would be challenged. He slipped into the cleaners changing room and put on the green uniform and Wellingtons. He pulled on a cap and gloves, half filled a bucket with water, picked up a mop and set off.

He managed to walk around the hospital without attracting any attention at all. It was as though he was invisible. At last he found the right room. Fortunately the young man was in a room on his own. He slipped the mask over his mouth and nose and went in. He came up to the young man who was in a kind of body brace. He looked into the young man's eyes and pulled down the mask and said,

"Can you answer me by blinking your eyes? Once for yes two for no?"

The young man blinked once.

"I am the Messenger of Death, have you heard of me?" A look of hope came into the young man's eyes and he blinked once.

"Have you need of me?" Tears streamed down the young man's face, and he blinked once.

"Then I will come on Sunday, after visiting hours, there will be less staff on, and also less chance of being discovered," he said, he looked at the chart at the end of the bed, "Will Hargreaves," he read, "Well my friend, I will be back on Sunday, you won't forget will you?"

Will blinked twice. The Messenger dried his eyes and told him not to despair, and left quickly as he heard someone coming down the corridor. On the way home he stopped off to get a copy of Will winning his race at the Olympics, and then he travelled on the train to Will's home while his family were at the television studios. He got into the house without setting off any alarms and stole Will's Olympic medal and a few other pieces and hastily left.

When he returned home he made his plan. Every detail must be in place, he could not risk failing this young man.

Chapter Nineteen
Jean's Return

Bland was having his breakfast when Jean walked in. He was still reading the black book and only had a couple of pages left. He had stayed up into the small hours determined to read the whole thing, and had fallen asleep with the book across his chest.

"Jean!" he said surprised, "You're back."

"Yes," she said, "it's the funeral tomorrow and I'm not missing that."

"You don't need to go to that," said Bland, " there will be a lot of people turning up, and some are out to make trouble."

"You'll be there won't you?"

"Yes but I'm on duty and won't be able to look after you."

"I'm going with other people so I'll be alright. Really Robert I'm not a child. I'm just going out to unload the car."

"Unload the car," he said, "what have you got in it?"

"Stuff from my house and clothes, I can't live out of a suitcase for ever. If you remember I left in a hurry and took nothing with me."

"Oh," said Bland, "do you need some help?"

"No," she said.

"Don't I even get a kiss?" he shouted after her as she disappeared out of the door.

"Only if you stop being silly about the funeral," she shouted back as she opened the boot of the car.

Bland put on his jacket, and tucked the book in his pocket; he had at last finished it. Ideas were formulating in his head, but he needed to check on a few people and verify his facts. He thought he knew who it was the Ivan the terrible might be.

Jean came staggering in carrying some really beautiful ball gowns. Bland took them from her and laid them out on the long table in the dining room.

"What are these for?" he asked.

"Queenie," said Jean, "I'm bringing in some more, I don't need them any more as there are a lot of bad memories associated with them."

Just at that moment Boyd turned up to collect Bland.

"Good morning Sir," he said, "going to the ball are we?"

"No we are not," said Bland irritated, "Jean is letting Queenie have them for her shop."

"Really," said Boyd, "they are beautiful".

"Come along Boyd, no time to fanny about, we are going to the west end if the Super agrees."

"Do I get a kiss," said Bland as Jean rushed past him her arms filled with more dresses.

"Oh if you must," she said on her return journey, and she gave him a quick peck on the cheek and rushed back to the car.

"How soon one gets taken for granted and pushed aside," said Bland as he and Boyd headed for the car.

"Yes Sir," said Boyd not wanting to pursue the subject, "why are we going to the west end?"

"I think I know who Ivan the Terrible is but I need to check my facts. I can't get any clues on this Messenger of Death, so we might as well do something else until we get the reports back from the security cameras people."

Boyd drove into the station and waited in the canteen while Bland went to see the Super.

Chapter Twenty
The Return of Big Harry

Teddy and Arthur put up the mirror that Quentin had just finished restoring, and stood well back to look at it. They both heaved a sigh of satisfaction it looked wonderful.

"You've done a real good job Quentin," said Teddy.

"It's the business," said Arthur. Quentin didn't answer; he was busy fiddling about with the lights above the mirror, and repositioning an Italian chandelier. He climbed gingerly down from the ladder and switched on the lights.

"There Uncle Teddy, what do you think of that?" Everything lit up. The chandelier threw out bright dancing rainbows that reflected in the mirror and on all the walls. The mirror-looked magic, as the rainbows of colour bounced off of every faceted edge, like a huge diamond. The chandelier swayed slightly because of the workshop door being opened and the breeze was filtering through, and the room danced with moving light.

"Oh very nice, very nice indeed," said a voice behind them. They turned to find Big Harry and two of his henchmen standing behind them, which explained the open door. Quentin gave a startled cry in his throat.

"Allo 'Arry," said Teddy calmly, "what brings you 'ere?"

"Well Teddy, I wouldn't want you to think that I 'ad anything to do with Louis being rubbed out"

"I never thought you 'ad, said Teddy, "a leading business man like you don't ruin 'is reputation murdering a scum bag like 'im."

"It's not that I didn't lean on 'im a little you understand, a little slap for being a naughty boy, made 'im see the error of 'is ways. Got 'im to understand which side of the river he belonged. When 'e left me him was alive, if a little battered."

"We 'eard that Myra Cambora, put a contract out on 'im," said Arthur

"Well there you are then," said Big Harry, "even little Arthur knows it wasn't me. Well Teddy not much longer until your opening. My lady wife is looking forward to it no end."

"Well," said Teddy, " we is nearly finished now. Quentin has just finished a cocktail cabinet for a client, why don't you come and have a look. I'd value your opinion." They all trooped into the warehouse and there it stood. The wood was a good mellow colour due to its age and shone from years of being polished. Teddy bent down and put a plug in the wall and switched it on.

"For the lights inside," he explained to Harry. He pulled the front flap down as though he was opening a bureau and then he opened two doors outwards, there was a whirring noise and the lights went on and the central part started to revolve and rise up, while it played a tinkling tune. It got to a certain height and stopped but the music played on. The inside was lined with mirrors and all the glasses and decanters sparkled.

"There is plenty of storage," said Teddy opening the bottom cupboards, "a couple of champagne buckets and an ice box." Big Harry was in his element.

"What are these crystal pots and dishes for?" he asked. Teddy didn't know, so he made it up. He was a beer and whiskey man himself – he had no time for the arty-farty stuff.

"Well 'Arry that's for your cherries, this is for lemon and lime slices, swizzle sticks in that pot and umbrellas in there. This is for the bits of stuff you put in Pimms, all the things that a discerning gentleman would want. It's not for the *Hoi Polloi*. I've got someone interested in it so it will probably be gone before opening day."

"Oh Teddy," said Big Harry, "my lady wife has been looking for something like this for ages, she 'as a lot of cocktail parties you know, but we 'aven't found nothin' like this. Look at these cocktail shakers. The music had stopped and Harry was exploring the contents. He found some swizzle sticks in one of the drawers, and in one compartment he found all the stainless steel tools you would need for making fancy cocktails.

Quentin slipped into the kitchen, he had six cocktail glasses in the classic V-shape, one of which was chipped; and he threw it away. He carefully washed the other five, and four he wrapped in tissue and placed in one of the galleries fancy boxes. The fifth he put in a box of it's own. He went back to the workshop

The cabinet contained lots of different glasses, but none like the ones that Quentin was holding out for Big Harry's approval. Teddy took the glasses from Quentin and took one out of the box, he gently unwrapped it and passed it to Harry,

" These is nice, but very expensive of course, they may be too much for you 'Arry."

While Quentin had been in the kitchen Teddy had sold the cabinet to Harry at a very, very good price. Harry also now paid top whack for the four glasses in their fancy box now being tied up with gold ribbons by Quentin. As soon as he finished tying up the glasses Quentin popped into the kitchen and came out with the last glass in its box.

"Trouble is Mr Harry," he said, "some of the guests that come to cocktail-parties can be right numpties, breaking glasses and things. Uncle Teddy always gives a spare glass free of charge to put away in case that happens. It's such a shame to spoil such an expensive set of glasses."

"That's right," said Teddy, "But that service is only for our most discerning clients. Thank-you for reminding me Quentin."

"Oh Teddy," said Big Harry handing over a large roll of money, "that's what I call real business, looking after your client. Thank-you Quentin," he said taking the glass.

They watched him and his henchmen pack the cabinet upright in the very large boot of his car and drive slowly out of the yard..

"'Ideous object," said Teddy, holding his hand out, Quentin slapped his hand down on top of Teddy's and said,

"The epitome of vulgarity and bad taste."

"It's gone to the right place," said Arthur slapping his hand down on top of theirs. They all threw their hands up in the air and shouted,

" YES, YES, YES," and burst into laughter.

"What a stroke of luck you thinking of those glasses," said Teddy.

"Well they weren't a complete set," said Quentin.

"I know," said Teddy, "but he paid over the odds for the complete set and only got four, and was grateful to get one free."

" It wasn't the kind of thing we could sell here," said Arthur.

"No Arfer, nothing but the best for us now," said Teddy, "no tat."

"You know we need something else for that window," said Quentin.

"Like what?" said Arthur.

"Dunno," said Quentin.

"What about Grannies old writing desk and foot stool?" said Arthur, we don't use it, and it's full of old photographs and papers. It slopes down at the front."

"You don't mean an old school desk," said Quentin horrified at the thought of an old desk in his shop.

"He means a Davenport," said Teddy, "she kept it a treat, it's in good nick."

"Lets go and see it," said Quentin, "come along Uncle Teddy, strike while the iron is hot." He opened the door and Teddy walked reluctantly through. He did not want to walk down the road with Quentin, because today Quentin had excelled himself. He was wearing pink satin flowing harem trousers with a shirt to match. Black, patent leather, Cuban heeled boots. A ground length, black flowing cloak, with a lime green silk lining. And to top it all a black hat with a plume running around the brim. He looked like a gay Chinese Zorro, all he was short of was the sword.

"Quentin," said Teddy as they walked down the road passing people who were staring open mouthed at them. Teddy tried not to notice them.

"Yes Uncle Teddy."

"When we open, me and Arfer and going to dress formally, you know, black tie and all that, it is after all a champagne do, and they will be all poshed up, especially 'Arry and 'is Missus."

"Me too," said Quentin, "black classic suit, plain white shirt and black tie, in keeping with the image we are trying to project." Teddy inwardly breathed a sigh of relief and poked his tongue out at a fat woman who was staring at them. She looked away and hurried off

When they got to the house, Teddy showed Quentin into the parlour, as Queenie called it.

"You look around and I'll go and make us a nice cup of tea," said Teddy and he disappeared down the hall to the kitchen. He got out the fine bone china, and the silver teapot, he poured milk into the little silver milk jug, the he put some sugar lumps into the elegant little silver sugar bowl, and placed the tongs on the tray. He put some digestive biscuits on a plate, and lemon slices in a glass dish, as he knew Quentin preferred lemon in his tea.

When the tea was made he carried the tray through to the parlour. Quentin jumped up and said,

"This house is a museum."

"Yer, that's what Arfer is always saying," said Teddy, "he wants to get rid of most of it and get some modern stuff."

"Never," said Quentin, "you have some wonderful stuff, the Davenport is in superb condition and I found all these wonderful photographs in the drawers.

"Oh yes," said Teddy, pouring the tea, "They are all of family going right back. I always meant to make up a large album, but somehow I never got around to it, and Arfer's not interested."

" Let me do it for you," said Quentin.

"You sure," said Teddy.

"Oh yes I'd love to do it."

"So you like the Davenport," said Teddy passing Quentin the biscuits.

"It's exquisite,"

"My old man always 'ad good stuff in the 'ouse, no rubbish."

"That's obvious," said Quentin, " there's one or two other pieces that I'd like to take, if you can bear to part with them."

"Which ones," said Teddy.

"The stool, as suggested by Uncle Arthur, the nest of tables, there's always a ready market for them, especially as new houses are so much smaller nowadays."

"Okay, we never use them."

"That bow fronted desk, and the French table lamp with the beads."

"Okay," said Teddy, but ask Arfer first because these things belong to both of us."

Quentin sipped his tea and gazed at the silver tea set on its beautiful silver tray. Teddy noticed his intense gaze and said quickly,

"The silver and the china stay, me and Arfur use it all the time."

As they walked back to the shop Teddy said,

"Quentin, I think you are a bit of a burglar."

"Why?"

"Because what was ours now seems to be yours."

"No harm trying Uncle Teddy, no harm trying."

They walked the rest of the way back to the shop in silence, Teddy reflecting that Quentin had a good eye for things, and apart from his taste in clothes he was a good lad.

Chapter Twenty-One
A Visit to M15

Bland and Boyd arrived at Andrew Middleton's office about three o' clock. He profiled people and events, and had a vast knowledge of the criminal world. His office was quiet, only one telephone, no computer or copier, in fact not a single gadget of the modern world. He had a wooden filing cabinet and wrote in long hand, for his secretary to put on the computer in her office at the other end of the corridor. She came into his office twice a day, once in the morning to bring him the previous days work in a leather folder and his mail, and once in the afternoon to pick up what he had done that day.

"Hello Robert, Sergeant," he said shaking hands with them, "tea is on its way," and he indicated that they should sit in the comfy armchairs at the other end of the office. Once they had settled Bland said,

"Look Andy I what you to read this book. I think I know who Ivan the Terrible is, but I need more information concerning the events I've written on this sheet of paper."

"Ah this is the famous black book," said Andrew taking it, "I seem to remember you being involved in one of the events involving a bent copper."

"I did indeed, " said Bland, and got shot for my trouble. I don't want to repeat the situation, so I'm treading very carefully this time."

"Give me a couple of days Robert and I'll have something for you – ah, here's tea, he said as his secretary came in with a laden tray. She placed it in front of Andrew and left.

He started to pour the tea and hand it around,

"Dig in chaps," he said, help yourselves, no standing on ceremony here."

"You treat yourself very well," said Bland, getting a plate and tucking into the sandwiches, as did Boyd.

"No point in starving yourself," said Andrew, "I find if I have a decent break now I can continue on until nine o' clock tonight, and then go home in the comparative quiet, not so many people on the road then."

"Don't you have a social life?" asked Boyd.

"Week-ends," said Andrew, "I go down to the country to play golf, ride, go to dinner with my friends and sometimes go to the Saturday night parties, but I'm getting too long in the tooth for that now as they go on all night. I also go skiing twice a year, go to friends in the Bahamas, and go to the Far East at least once a year. I love the Orient."

"Oh," said Boyd, thinking that in comparison to Andrew's life, he had been leading a very dull life up until now.

Andrew suddenly jumped up and rushed out of the office. Bland and Boyd looked at each other in surprise. A couple of minutes later he was back carrying a very large gift-wrapped parcel covered in curly ribbons and bows.

"Here you are Robert," he said, plonking it down in front of Bland, who just managed to whip his cup and saucer and plate out of the way in time.

"It's your wedding present. Congratulations, and don't open it until you get home. In my experience the ladies like to be the one who opens gifts."

"Well," said Bland surprised, "thank-you very much Jean will be delighted." They chatted on for about another half hour, and then Bland and Boyd got up to leave. They told Andrew that they had to get back for a meeting. They were policing a funeral the next day and the Super wanted to make sure that everybody was in the right place, especially as the parents were being allowed out of custody to attend.

"Rather you than me old boy," said Andrew shaking hands with them.

"You'd rather watch it unfold from here looking down from your ivory tower," said Bland.

"You know what they say Robert, the onlooker sees most of the game and its very true."

"Well at least you don't get shot," said Bland.

"My point exactly," said Andrew laughing.

As they walked down the corridor Bland gave Boyd his parcel to carry, and Boyd thanked his lucky stars that it wasn't any larger.

When they got back to the office people were milling about all over the place. Two of the larger detectives were to guard Johnny Oates and two of the more well upholstered and stronger policewomen were to guard Fanny. The Super was convinced they would try and make a break for freedom as soon as they could.

Bland and Boyd were in the security ring around the two, to protect them from the public, other plain-clothes officers were to be dotted around in the church and in the crowd outside.

Eventually the Super was satisfied that everybody knew what he or she had to do, and everyone went thankfully home.

Chapter twenty-two
Beth's Funeral

Bland was up early and so was Jean. By the time he was showered and dressed breakfast was cooked. Just as he sat down to his bacon and eggs the front door bell rang.

"I'll get it," said Jean, "its only Boyd."

"You're early," said Bland, when Boyd appeared

" I called him earlier and suggested he have breakfast with us," said Jean, "you were in the shower."

"Oh," said Bland. Boyd sat down and Jean put a large breakfast down in front of him, and his eyes lit up.

"Thanks Mrs. Bland," he said and tucked in.

"The Super is attending the funeral," said Bland, "a wreath has been sent."

"That's a bit unusual isn't it Sir?" said Boyd.

"Yes, but he thinks its good public relations, especially as we haven't found the killer yet."

"I think its disgraceful," said Jean, "he's using the funeral to his own ends."

"You're not going are you Jean?" asked Bland.

94

"Indeed I am," she said pouring everybody a second cup of coffee, "don't worry I'm going with someone. I'll be perfectly all right."

"Could get rough Mrs Bland," said Boyd.

"That's what I keep telling her," said Bland, "but will she listen."

"No, she won't," said Jean and began to bustle about clearing the table.

"Abigail Merchant is going," said Boyd.

"What to the funeral?" said Bland.

"No she wants to be part of the security ring, with us Sir, wants to get involved, get a feel of the mood of the people."

"What utter nonsense," said Bland, "she will only get in the way, anyway the Super wouldn't allow it would he?"

"Says she going with, or without his say so."

"It's a pity she didn't get involved sooner," said Jean when the child really needed her."

"Well you know what it is Sir," said Boyd, "she fancies you, everybody knows it but you."

"Oh really," said Jean bristling. Bland sighed and thought, well done Boyd; you always open your mouth before you brains in gear.

Come along Boyd," he said jumping up, got to get to the early morning meeting. Good-bye Darling," he shouted at Jean, making for the front door. Jean sprang up between them and the front door, her eyes flashing, hands on hips.

"Anxious to see her are we?" she hissed, "your are not this eager to get to work usually."

"It's the funeral," said Bland lamely.

"Do I get a kiss?" she said sweetly, much too sweetly for Bland's taste.

"Of course dear," he said. He lightly kissed her on her forehead, dodged around her, and made a bolt for the door with Boyd hot on his heels. They jumped in the car and roared down the drive and into the traffic.

"Boyd, when will you ever learn?"

"I know Sir I'm so sorry."

"Its not true is it, about Abigail?"

"Oh yes Sir, she really has the hots for you."

"Oh really Boyd – just drive." They sped on to the station in silence. Bland could only think of how much he loved Jean, especially with her flashing eyes.

. . . .

Mrs Mercer was sitting by her granddaughter's small coffin. The funeral people had arrived and they were about to take the coffin and place it in the glass carriage. The top of the coffin was covered with white lilies, and the bearers lifted the coffin with no effort at all and walked slowly down the stairs followed by Mrs Mercer. Once the coffin was in place and all the floral tributes had been arranged around it, she locked the front door and then took her place in the back of the black limousine. A small lonely figure, she was the only family mourner. The leader at the front struck his staff on the ground, and started to move forward slowly. The two black horses pulling the carriage surged forward nodding their heads, and set off slowly, followed by the silent running of the limousine. People in the street stood silent as the cortege passed them, and some of the older generation bowed their heads, and removed their hats as a mark of respect. That's, as it should be, thought Mrs Mercer as they passed slowly by. As they got closer to the church she could see a large crowd pushing and jostling, being held back by the police. It was really noisy, the Oates had just been taken into the church handcuffed to their escorts and people were shouting abuse. Suddenly a large man jumped up onto the church wall, he was a local trader, who owned a stall in the market nearby.

"Now," he shouted, "this is a little girl's funeral, so show proper respect and silence, that means everyone or I'll want to know the reason why. Until she is laid to rest I don't want to 'ear another sound." The crowd went silent, not a sound was made, and all that could be heard was the distant traffic, and the clip-clop of the horses' hooves as they came up to the church gate. Beth's coffin was gently lifted out of the carriage, and taken into the church followed by her grandmother. She glared at the Oates as she passed them. They should not be here, she thought, they didn't care about Beth, all they could see was an opportunity to escape.

After the church service, the coffin was taken to the grave in a quiet corner of the graveyard. The ground around the grave was covered with floral tributes. When it was over Mrs Mercer and a couple of her close friends were escorted to the car and were driven home. They were to have lunch together in memory of Beth.

Meanwhile a scuffle broke out and the Oates made a bid for freedom, but they were handcuffed to their escorts, and after some unseemly rolling about on the ground, the police handcuffed their hands behind their backs and dragged them struggling towards the prison van waiting.

Although the ring of protection was around them the angry crowd surge forward and started to pelt them with rotten fruit and vegetables supplied by the man who had brought the crowd to order before the funeral

Bland and Boyd were close to Oates and trying to dodge the missiles being thrown at them. Abigail suddenly appeared and flung herself in front of Bland, stretching out her arms and leaning on Bland, screaming at the crowd to get back..

"That's her," said Jean to Queenie, and Queenie hurled an overripe melon at Abigail and it found its mark. It ran down her neck and inside her dress.

"Right in the kisser," shouted Queenie. Jean took aim and fired, unfortunately Abigail jumped out of the way, screaming and jumping up and down. The rotten stinking melon had slid down inside her clothes and was now dripping out of the bottom of her dress. She was beside herself with rage. Jeans rotten tomatoes found a mark all right, but not Abigail but Bland's chest. There was a loud splat and Bland looked up.

"Jean," he exclaimed in disbelief. Jean and Queenie beat a hasty retreat. The tomatoes slipped down inside his jacket and he could feel his crutch getting wet. Then there was a splodge, the tomatoes had run down his trouser legs and landed on his well polished shoes. He gazed down on them in dismay.

"Boyd," he shouted, "go to the newsagents over the road and get me two newspapers."

"Which ones?" asked Boyd.

"I'm not going to read they Boyd, I want them to sit on in the car, so get thick and large ones. Now hurry."

The Oates were now incarcerated in the prison van, and were whisked off to prison with a large crowd running after them, still hurling rotten fruit and veg. Things suddenly went quiet and while Bland waited for Boyd to return, he shook the tomatoes off his shoes. His trousers were now sticking to him and his shirt seemed to have clued itself to his chest. It was bloody awful. Boyd returned with the newspapers and they made their way to the car.

"Now Boyd spread them all over the seat and on the floor where my feet are going to go, then get me home as quick as you can."

"What about the Super's press conference?"

"Bugger the Super and his press conference, just get me home." Boyd got Bland back to his house as quickly as possible without having an accident or running foul of the law.

"Drop me at the front door and then go and park at the top of the drive," said Bland. As they got to the front door Bland leap out, and rushed into the front door which had been opened by Jean. Bland found himself standing on a huge sheet of plastic.

"What's this for?" he said.

"Get all your clothes off," said Jean, "including your shoes, you can't go around the house making a mess and stinking up the place, come along, every stitch."

"You're insatiable woman," shouted Bland, getting off the now cold smelly and clingy clothes.

"All your clean clothes are laid out ready, warm towels are on the rail so get upstairs and have a shower. I'm sorry about the tomatoes, they were meant for Abigail."

"I could see that," shouted Bland as he race naked, two steps at a time up the stairs.

Just at that moment Boyd came in. He saw Bland disappearing up the stairs and shouted,

"Looking for your red satin sequined thong Sir?" He heard Bland swear and the bathroom door slam, and then he saw Jean and the smile faded from his face.

"Well Darren, " said Jean smiling, "could you help me carry these clothes through to the utility room? so that I can sort out which needs to go to the dry cleaners and which can be washed. You take those two corners and I'll take these." They walked the plastic through into the utility room and left it on the floor.

"Come and have some coffee and sandwiches, its all ready." They sat at the kitchen table and Jean poured the coffee and said,

"What's all this about a red satin sequined thong?"

"Oh its nothing Mrs Bland, its just a joke," said Boyd feeling that he had put his foot in it again.

"Well share the joke," said Jean. There was an uncomfortable silence as Boyd tried to think of something to say, and mercifully he heard Bland coming down the stairs. He immediately jumped up and thanked Jean for the coffee and sandwiches and told her that they had to go because the Super's conference was in eight minutes.

"Ah coffee and sandwiches," said Bland rubbing his hands together.

"No time for that Sir," said Boyd, "the press conference starts in eight minutes." The doorbell rang and Jean got up to answer it.

Come along Darling," she said, "time to get back. I'll make you something special tonight." Bland grabbed a sandwich; as Jean and Boyd propelled him towards the door. Jean opened the door and Queenie and Quentin burst in.

"In there," said Jean pointing to the dining room and the pair of them rushed in. Quentin screamed at the top of his voice,

"Oh my God, oh my God."

"You know what Boyd?" said Bland.

"No Sir," said Boyd.

"It really **IS** time to go."

They made their way to the car at the top of the drive, and the last thing Jean heard as she closed the door was,

"Oh really Boyd, you might have removed theses newspapers."

"Sorry Sir."

Chapter twenty-Three
The Press Conference

When Bland and Boyd arrived back at the station, the Superintendent was in full flood, in front of the cameras. Not only were there newspapermen jostling for position, but also the television news people had turned up.

"We are not needed here," said Bland, "let's go to the canteen for a quiet cuppa, especially as I've had no lunch, then we can go back to the office and get some paperwork done. I need to make some telephone calls, and if the Super doesn't have any other ideas we'll go home early."

"Will we have to go to the tramps funeral?" asked Boyd.

"You and I will Boyd, if only to see who else attends. Killers usually go to the funerals of those they have killed, even if they view from a distance."

"I guess it will be a quiet affair Sir?"

"Yes, there doesn't seem to be any family except his brother who has come down from Scotland. Although he was initially identified by the doctor in the first instance, the brother came down to officially identify him and arrange his funeral."

The canteen was empty; everyone was outside listening to the Super waffle on. Greta, behind the counter, asked them what they wanted and Bland ordered apple pie with cream, and a cup of coffee, and Boyd had a Coke.

"When is the funeral Sir," asked Boyd as they sat down.

"Monday at eleven o'clock," answered Bland tucking into his apple pie

"Do you reckon the Messenger will strike again Sir?"

"Oh yes Boyd, there are many people who he will see as needing his services."

"We are never going to find him are we Sir?"

"Could be a her," mused Bland, "although I very much doubt it. Rest assured Boyd we will find the Messenger, it will just take a little longer than usual."

The canteen door slammed open and Abigail stormed in.

"Robert," she said, still angry and bursting to get her own back, "did you see that crazy woman this morning?"

"Which particular crazy did you have in mind? You were spoilt for choice this morning," said Bland, "they were all there to pelt the Oates with rotten fruit"

"Oh no, no indeed," said Abigail getting up a full head of steam, "that fat old tart I know – that's Queenie Hugget and she aimed at me pacifically. I heard her shout 'right in the kisser' why would she do that? I've never done anything to her."

"Perhaps you did something to one of her friends," said Boyd. Bland threw him a warning glance and Boyd said no more.

"What do you mean? One of her friends?" demanded Abigail.

"What he means," said Bland quickly, "is that being in welfare and having a lot of contact with the more needy, and sometimes the downright nasty, you may have inadvertently upset someone. Its like police work, it's the nature of the game." Bland had chosen his words very carefully.

"What about that crazy bitch next to her?"

"I took the brunt of that missile," said Bland wincing at the thought.

"I know," said Abigail defiantly, "but it was meant for me and I dodged out of the way in time."

"Well thank-you very much," said Bland getting up, "letting me be covered with your rotten tomatoes."

"Oh Robert I didn't mean it," she said tearfully rolling her eyes at him.

The canteen doors were flung open and the Super marched in.

"You here again," he said to Abigail, "I could hear you screeching up the end of the corridor. I must say that it is a very poor show, you interfering with the ring of protection this morning, and then shouting at the crowd and whipping them up into frenzy, so that my officers were pelted with rotten fruit. It was most irresponsible of you. I shall be showing my displeasure by mentioning this incident to your department." He turned his back on her and said,

"You alright Robert?"

"Yes Sir."

"Good, put the bill for the dry cleaning on your expenses. Come to my office in about ten minutes and we'll share a glass." Abigail had worked herself up into a red- hot rage now.

"You pompous old windbag," she shouted.

"Oh you still here?" he said turning around.

"Call yourself a policeman? You couldn't find the Messenger of Death if he was kneeling on your chest about to strangle you. YOU, YOU first class, chromium plated, arsehole." She flounced out of the canteen letting the swing doors slam behind her.

"Unhinged," said the Super and then he wandered back down the corridor to his own office whistling 'Be Happy' and called back,

"See you in ten minutes Robert," and could still be heard whistling as he turned into his office.

When he had gone Boyd said,

"Boy was she ever mad, especially when the Super blamed her for the whole incident."

"And to that end Boyd, she must never find out that it was Jean. Do you catch my drift?"

"Oh yes Sir, mums the word."

"Right back to the office Boyd and then I'll go along and see what he wants."

Chapter Twenty-Four
Meanwhile. . . . .

Queenie and Quentin arrived back at the Galleries with the booty they had collected from Jean.

"There's not enough room to display them," said Quentin in a panic.

"We need next door," said Queenie, "its just right, on the corner with that massive bay window going right around. Your uncle will have to buy it."

"Where is he?" said Quentin wringing his hands.

"Up at that bloody allotment I wouldn't wonder," said Queenie

"We have to go up and see him right now," said Quentin.

"Right," said Queenie, "we'll look in the pub on the way past and make sure 'e ain't in there."

Teddy and Arthur were indeed up at the allotment. They had been getting the beds and greenhouses ready for the winter. It was well into autumn now. Teddy usually tended the allotments on his own, as it was his domain. He liked the peace and quiet, but Arthur had insisted on coming with him today and he worked strictly under supervision. Teddy had a very large bunch of gigantic spring onions wrapped in newspapers that he was taking down to the local Chinese restaurant. They loved them; the ones they bought in the supermarket were too small and tasteless.

Teddy was locking up the huts when Arthur said,

"Someone's coming up the hill."

"Who is it?" asked Teddy.

"Dunno, looks like a group but I think its only two." Teddy tucked the spring onions under his arms and they both started downhill.

"Its Queenie and Quentin," said Arthur.

"So it is," said Teddy, "wonder what is so urgent that they 'ad to come up 'ere?"

They all met about half way down the hill. Queenie and Quentin both started talking at once. It was impossible to hear what either of they were saying.

"Quentin," shouted Queenie.

"Yes Auntie Queenie."

"Let me tell it."

"Yes Auntie Queenie."

"Teddy you've got to buy the unit next door. We've got all those wonderful gowns from Jean, Mr Bland's wife, and nowhere to display them.

"Can't buy it," said Teddy, "Because its already sold."

Quentin screamed, "Oh no, Auntie Queenie what are we going to do?"

"Teddy, make them an offer," said Queenie.

"Who do you think I am – the Godfather," said Teddy, "anyway I've already bought it. I bought it when I doubled the unit for Steve so 'e could 'ave a gallery and a workshop. There's no flat above because the unit's on the corner but there is storage. I suggest you 'ave your big old sewing machine in there so that you have more room in your flat. There's a small kitchen at the back but no space outside, only a tiny courtyard for your bins and of course the fire escape. The only upside is the big bay windows that go right around the corner.

"Just right for displaying gorgeous gowns," said Quentin, clasping his hands together. They hand now reached the bottom of the hill.

"I'll buy you a pint," said Teddy heading for the pub.

"No you won't," said Queenie, "you'll buy me a large gin and tonic, several in fact."

"I'll have a long slow screw against the wall," said Quentin.

"No you won't," said Teddy, "this is a pub, not a cocktail bar, anyway I ain't askin' for it."

"Very well," said Quentin, sniffing on his large silk hanky, "I'll have a vodka and orange."

"Right," said Teddy, "Arfer, you get the drinks in and we'll go and grab that table in the corner, over there, out of the way." A lot of customers stared at Quentin, so he stared back and they looked away embarrassed and got on with their drinks. If he was with Teddy and Arthur he must be all right.

They all got settled and Arthur came back with a tray loaded down with drinks, nuts, crisps, cheeses rolls and hot sausage rolls. He and Teddy hadn't had any lunch so he presumed that everybody was hungry.

"Teddy," said Arthur, "Chan's over there, give me them onions and I'll give them to him, to take back to the Palace of the Blue Dragon.."

"Righto Arfer," said Teddy, handing them over.

"Now," he said turning to Queenie, "get in touch with Sammy and he'll take down that partition between the two units, it's not a load bearing wall, then you'll have one big area. Quentin I suppose we can rely on you to organise the décor and lighting?"

"Of course," said Quentin, nibbling on a hot sausage roll. Arthur came back with a half bottle of champagne.

"Chan sent this over for the onions, I told 'im it wasn't necessary but 'e insisted."

"Give it to Quentin," said Teddy, "can't mix it with beer, it gives you gas."

"Someone of discernment at last," said Quentin, "I suppose it's too much to ask for a champagne glass in here?"

Teddy called the barmaid over and asked her to open the bottle and get a glass. She came back a moment later with the bottle opened and a Babysham glass.

Teddy brought out a large bunch of keys, took some off the ring and gave them to Queenie and Quentin.

"We open in a weeks time Quentin, do you reckon that it will be ready in time?"

"Of course," said Quentin, I shall work day and night."

"You could always open the new shop after the opening."

"Never," said Queenie and Quentin together.

"Suit yourselves," said Teddy.

"Pity you ain't got no other bits, said Arthur.

"What bits?" said Queenie.

"You know, the bits that ladies 'ave to 'ave to match, like shoes and 'ats and bags, that sort of thing."

"You're so right, " said Quentin, "dear Uncle Arthur."

"Considering that you 'ave never bin married," said Teddy, "you seem to know a lot about what ladies like."

"I've 'ad me moments," said Arthur, "even though I've never been actually married."

"You sly old dog," said Quentin, giggling into his champagne.

" That's why you ain't married now Teddy," said Queenie, "cos you don't know what ladies like."

"Careful Queenie," said Teddy, "I've just given you a new shop."

Queenie ignored him and sipped on her gin and tonic and delicately nibbled on some nuts.

"Jean," she said suddenly, "Jean might 'ave some, we'll go and see 'er later."

"You cant go barging into the Chief Inspector's 'ouse and ask for 'is wife's second 'and bits," said a scandalized Teddy.

"I ain't coming," said Arthur.

"Neither would I if I 'ad any sense in me 'ead," said Teddy, "but I've got to make sure that these two don't pester the Chief Inspector."

"I still ain't coming, muttered Arthur.

Chapter Twenty-Five
Words with the Super and Dinner Guests

Bland wandered down the corridor to see the Superintendent. He wondered what he wanted this time. He tapped on the door and went in.

"Come in Robert and sit down," said the Super, getting up to get their drinks. He opened a small cabinet and brought out a bottle of good sipping whiskey and poured two generous glasses and handed one to Bland. They both said 'cheers' and took a large quaff from their glasses and leaned back in their chairs content.

"Well Robert I'm glad the child's funeral is over. The next one should attract less attention. I was right about the Oates making a bid for freedom."

"You certainly were Sir," said Boyd.

"Anything new to report?"

"No Sir, we hope to get a report tomorrow about what's been picked up on the CCTV cameras. It's a slim hope but you never know what might turn up."

" True Robert, do you think he'll strike again?"

"Unfortunately yes Sir."

"So do I Robert, do you think he's local?"

"Oh yes Sir, he wouldn't have been able to travel far with no number plates."

"My thoughts exactly, did you get a chance to read those extracts in the black book?"

"Yes Sir, I read the whole book and I think I've got an inkling as to who Ivan the Terrible might be, but I'm not committing myself yet. I've got Andrew Middleton confirming some of the information for me, and looking up events. He's going to give me a profile on Tuesday which will confirm whether I'm right or wrong."

"Good man," said the Super, "I guess it's a waiting game now Robert, always the hardest part, keep me informed. I'll be interested to see what Andrew Middleton has to say," he gazed through his crystal glass admiring the colour of the whiskey as it shone through the facets in the glass,

"Press call went well this morning," he said at last.

"Indeed Sir,"

"Have to keep on the right side of the public Robert, after all we are the servants of the people."

"Indeed Sir," said Bland," knowing that the Super was servant to no one, rather they his." They both downed the last drops of whiskey and placed their glasses on the desk.

"Well Robert I wont keep you, I expect you have things to do."

"Yes Sir," said Bland getting up and going to the door, as he opened it to leave the Super said,

"I don't think it would be wise to let that Merchant woman know who the crazy woman was, do you Robert?"

"No Sir," said Bland and quietly closed the door behind him as he left and went back to his office.

As he and Boyd drove home that evening he reflected that very little got past the Super. He was a wily old bugger, a bit like a fox. Boyd drove up to the front door and Bland climbed out of the car stiffly and was heading towards the front door when Boyd called out,

Aren't you going to take your present Sir? It's been in the car since yesterday, you know the one that Andrew Middleton gave you, it's in the boot."

"Good grief Boyd I'd forgotten all about it." He opened the boot and collected his parcel, said good night to Boyd and went inside.

"I'm home," he called as he placed the present and his keys on the hall table. Jean came from the direction of the kitchen.

"Hello Darling," she said, giving him a kiss, "the flowers are lovely, thank-you so much." Bland had phoned the flower shop; during the afternoon, he had felt in view of all that had happened that day, Jean deserved some flowers.

They went into the dining room and there were six places laid for dinner, and all the best china and silver were out. The flowers were in the centre of the table and looked lovely. Bland made a mental note that he would be using that florist again.

"Who's coming to dinner? Boyd never mentioned anything."

"He's not coming," said Jean, "Queenie phoned me this afternoon, they should be here any minute now."

"They?"

"Yes Dear, Queenie, Quentin, Teddy and Arthur."

"What do they want?" asked Bland

"I'm sure I don't know," said Jean, "but we will soon find out."

"Oh well," sighed Bland and shrugged his shoulders, "by the way there's a wedding present on the table in the hall. It's from Andrew Middleton, I've had it since yesterday."

"Oh Robert, really, he'll wonder why we haven't thanked him yet." They went into the hall and Jean took off the ribbons and bows and unwrapped it. Inside was a large white box with the word Lalique emblazoned in black on it.

"Oh Robert," said Jean as she lifted the lid off and laid it to one side, she carefully separated the tissue and gently lifted out a splendid Lalique vase.

"Oh Robert," said Jean again, "it's just beautiful, see how the light shines through."

"I once saw it described as polar bears breath," said Bland, its such a unique glass."

"It must have cost the earth," said Jean.

"He's very rich," said Bland, "has a huge estate in the country." Jean placed it on the long sideboard in the dining room and took the wrappings into the kitchen. Bland went upstairs to wash and change before their guests arrived, and Jean saw to the finishing touches to the canapés and nibbles for the pre dinner drinks.

A few minutes later Bland was back looking very smart.

"Anything I can do?"

"No Darling just see to the drinks when they get here."

The doorbell rang, which made they both jump as they were lost in their own thoughts. Bland opened the door and there stood Teddy and a very reluctant Arthur and Queenie and Quentin, all dressed in their best. Queenie had seen to that.

"Welcome," said Bland, "come on in." Jean came forward and welcomed everybody.

"I'm sorry about this Mrs Bland," said Teddy, "but they would insist on coming."

"Not me," muttered Arthur

"Nonsense," said Jean, "come in dinner is nearly ready". She ushered them into the sitting room and they stood there feeling sheepish and uncomfortable.

"Robert dear, you get everybody a drink and I'll check on the dinner."

Bland took their coats and put them on the hat stand in the hall. He came back and slapped his hands together saying,

"Now what is everybody drinking? Teddy? Arthur? What would you say to a glass of bitter? I've got a barrel in the utility room."

"Yes please," they said in unison and Arthur looked a little happier.

"Now Queenie and Quentin, I know Jean has wine to go with the meal but what would you like to start with. We've got sherry, gin and tonic, vodka, and I know Jean has made some champagne cocktails for those who like them, or perhaps you'd like dry martinis, we've got practically anything you can think of."

"I'd like a champagne cocktail," said Queenie."

"So would I," said Quentin.

Bland went to get the beer and Jean came in with the champagne cocktails.

"Blimey that was quick," said Teddy.

"Not that quick Teddy, " said Jean, "I guessed that's what Quentin and Queenie would like and had them ready." Bland appeared carrying a tray, on which was three large glasses of beer, which he handed around.

"Now," said Jean, "what's this all about?"

"Well," said Teddy, "Queenie was wondering…" and he trailed of.

"Nothing to do with me," muttered Arthur quietly.

"Well," said Quentin, "we were just wondering if …" and he also trailed off.

"Oh for heavens sake," said Queenie, "Arthur was wondering if you 'ad any bits?"

"Don't blame me," said Arthur.

"Bits?" said Jean mystified, "what kind of bits?"

"Well," said Queenie, "Teddy 'as bought a new shop with a big bow glass front to display the lovely gowns you so kindly gave me, and we were wondering if you 'ad any bits that you would like to get rid of?" Jean looked puzzled.

"Accessories," said Arthur, "'ats and bags and shoes."

"As a matter of fact I do," said Jean, "I have lots that I want to get rid of, that's if you can take it all."

"I reckon that we've got a bloody cheek to ask," said Teddy.

"Do we still get dinner?" asked Arthur. Jean and Bland burst out laughing,

"Of course," said Bland, "now lets sit down and have our dinner, I for one am starved."

It was a happy and jolly evening. It was arranged that they would all go down to Jean's house the following day to collect what Jean wanted to get rid of, all except Bland, he had to work. He wanted to see those CCTV reports; anyway he wasn't into accessories. He wondered if Jean would regret giving away all those very expensive clothes. He knew he couldn't possible buy her clothes like that, not on a coppers pay.

Later when their guests had gone home, Jean wrote a thank-you note to Andrew and they settled down to dream in front of the fire and unwind before they went to bed.

"Happy," said Bland putting his arm around Jean and pulling her closer.

"You can't know how happy I am Robert, to be able to have dinner and drinks and a few laughs and know that he's not waiting in the shadows to abuse me in some way. Getting rid of the clothes he bought me is clearing him out of my life. I want nothing left of him except David. Tomorrow will give me great joy."

Chapter Twenty-Six
Telling Pictures

Bland and Boyd arrived early the following morning. There were reports on Bland's desk but nothing that really interested him.

Constable Hathaway came in and gave Boyd what looked like a small cheap disposable cigarette lighter only thinner and flatter.

"Thanks Brian," said Boyd.

"It's just the bits we thought might be of interest to you, not a lot there really."

"Thanks anyway," said Boyd and Hathaway left the office. Boyd fitted the stick into his laptop and clicked and up came some film from the CCTV cameras. The first was from the garage near where the Oates lived.

"Look at this Sir," said Boyd. Bland looked over Boyd's shoulder.

"Is that coming from that little piece of plastic?"

"Yes Sir,"

"Wonders will never cease."

On the screen was a black limousine drawing up to the end pump. Someone dressed in sports gear got out of the car. The hood on the top was pulled well down over his face. He filled up the car and then went to pay.

"I wonder how he paid," said Bland. The film had now changed to the inside of the garage.

"Cash Sir, you can see him getting it out of his wallet - look there at the cash desk."

"I wonder if the cashier recognised him?" said Bland.

"Shouldn't think so," said Boyd, "they didn't speak to each other."

"Never mind," said Bland, "we'll still ask the question. We'll drop in on the garage later."

The next clip showed the car turning up the main street, near the Galleries. The cameras were larger there and could move and track, as the pictures went straight through to the traffic centre so they could control the traffic lights and ease the flow of traffic.

"Look at that Sir, you can just see the car turning to the left."

"So you can Boyd, I think we'll drive around that area and have a look around. Can we see the name of the road it turned into?"

Boyd spent minute or so homing in on the area, and sharpening the picture.

"Odd," said Boyd.

"What's odd?" said Bland.

"Well you wouldn't go up there unless you had business there, its one of those roads that you turn into, do a half circle and come back out on the same road again."

"Out of camera range," said Bland.

"Christ I never thought of that," said Boyd.

"He's smart and he's local to the area," said Bland, "well come along Boyd, let's be off." Boyd closed his laptop and put it in the case and slung it over his shoulder

"We'll drop the stick off to Brian on our way out," said Boyd

"What happens if we need to look at it again Boyd?"

"I've down loaded it onto the lap top Sir."

"Well done Boyd, well done."

They went to the garage first and showed a print of the Messenger to the cashier; he said he didn't know who it was,

"Don't look at faces mate, only look at 'ands, to see 'ow they are going to pay. Don't take credit cards or cheques anymore, too many bleeders ripped us off. Its cash only, they've just put up a notice up to that effect on the wall outside. Can't 'elp yer mate."

"Useless article," said Boyd as the got back into the car. They followed the route that the messenger had taken and Boyd was right, the road did go around in a half circle and rejoin the main road further on. They drove on for a short while and then Bland said,

"Let's go back Boyd, we have no idea what we are looking for and he's hardly likely to be driving around on a Saturday with no number plates."

"No Sir," said Boyd.

When they got back to the office there was a huge file on Bland's desk. It was the material collected for the case against the Oates. They had found out that he was collecting benefits from four different offices under the names of people who were dead. There was also robbery with violence; assault and they had both been picked up many times for being drunk and disorderly. As for Beth, the social services had many times tried to find them. They child was not registered with any doctor or school. Nobody had ever seen her. Bland couldn't help feeling that there were very serious faults in the system. People have children who don't deserve them he thought. It had always been a regret for him and his first wife that they had never had a child. To him it was as though Beth had been thrown away, despised and unwanted. He felt the anger rising in his chest and shuffled his papers to look at something else to take his mind off of Beth.

Bland phoned William Johnson's doctor at Guys and asked if he could come to see him. The doctor said yes, he was at present at his morning clinic, but if Bland came after lunch about one thirty, he would be free then.

Bland and Boyd went to lunch and on to the hospital. The nurse ushered them into the doctor's office, announcing them as though she was reading out the names of criminals in a law court.

"Do come in," the doctor said rising to shake hands, "please sit down and tell me what I can do for you."

It's about Willy Johnson as I mentioned on the phone," said Bland, "we are trying to piece together the last few days before his death. Did he mention staying with a friend?"

"As a matter of fact he did. We tried to get him into a local hospice but he refused to go. Then he came in for his medication and said he was going to stay with an old friend. It was someone he had known most of his life. We were really happy because it meant he was at last off the streets. He was suffering considerable pain by this time. He did not have much time left."

"I suppose he never mentioned the name or address of who he was going to stay with, " said Boyd.

"No," said the doctor but it was within walking distance from the hospital."

"Well," said Bland, "I'm sorry to have bothered you doctor I know how busy you are."

"Don't mention it," said the doctor, "I'm only sorry that I couldn't be more help." They left the doctor's office and walked slowly back to the car.

"What now Sir," asked Boyd.

"Back to the office," said Bland, "and we'll start preparing the case against the Oates. I'd like to see them banged up for good."

"Me too." said Boyd.

Chapter Twenty-Seven
Sunday Comes At Last.

Bland went down to Haversham Saturday night to be with Jean and the boys.

During the day Jean had filled Teddy and Arthur's van up with all the stuff that she wanted to get rid of.

"If you don't want it Queenie," she said, "just dump it."

"I don't think so," said Queenie, "I have a ready market for everything here, look won't you let me pay you? Its such good stuff."

"Certainly not," said Jean, "I am so glad to get rid of it all, you are doing me a favour."

"Don't want to be personal or nuffin but I 'eard you late 'usband was a right royal bastard."

"You could say that," sighed Jean, "he was vicious and cruel, not only to me, but as I found out later, there were others who suffered at his hands but he paid in the end, so there's an end to it."

Mr Bland is all right though ain't he? We think 'e's a prince among men."

"Do you really?" said Jean, "you are so right, he's wonderful, my only regret is that we never go together sooner."

"Oh 'ow lovely," said Queenie, and Quentin who was ear wigging in the background, quietly packing things in boxes could be heard sniffing into his handkerchief.

"Don't be upset Quentin," said Jean, "everything is all right now." Quentin buried his face in his handkerchief and rushed out of the room.

"Don't worry about 'im," said Queenie, "he'll be all right, Teddy puts it down to 'is artistic temperament."

Jean gave Queenie a list of how much each item had cost so that she could charge a fair price, some items had never been worn and still had the labels on.

By the time Bland arrived they had gone and Jean was alone.

"David and Seth not in.?" said Bland.

"Not yet," said Jean, "they've gone up to London. Seth has a show at the club tonight. It will probably be breakfast time before we see them." Good, thought Bland, an evening to ourselves.

Sunday morning came and they were enjoying a leisurely breakfast when the boys appeared one at a time in their dressing gowns. The smell of breakfast being cooked had brought them to the table.

David arrived first and flopped down in a chair at the table. Jean got up and dished up his breakfast.

"Thanks Mum, this is a real treat. Seth and I never bother."

"I could tell that, " said Jean, by the lack of food in the house. I had to do a big shop yesterday. How did the show go last night?"

"Oh Seth is just great. He's the best that they have got. The audiences just seem love him."

"Do I hear my name mentioned?" said Seth as he came in and flopped down at the table. Jean gave him his breakfast.

"Yes," she said, "but its all good."

"How long before you go to America," said Bland, "will you manage to go to the opening of the Galleries?"

"Yes," said David, "but Seth has to leave that night."

"Why don't they stay with us Jean? Until they both go to America. When do you expect to go David?"

"Thursday week actually," said David, "the date has been brought forward."

"Well," said Bland, "I've got to go back tonight, but you could stay on Jean for a couple of days, and come back with the boys."

"Great," said David and Seth together.

"Good," said Jean, "I can make sure the house is properly locked up."

"We always make sure that the front door is locked," said David and Seth nodded in agreement.

"What about the back door," said Jean, "when I came back yesterday the back door was unlocked and the alarm wasn't on." Seth and David looked sheepishly at each other.

. . . .

While they were chatting over breakfast, in London the Messenger was planning his day. He was to travel by train and he would not use taxis in case he was recognised later. He packed a large sports bag with things he needed for the hospital, and wearing a tracksuit with a hooded top he set off. He set off just before lunch, as he did not want to arrive too early. He had a meal in the station, and then bought his ticket, and waited for his train to arrive.

When the train came into Waterloo Station it was already quite crowded, which surprised the Messenger as it was Sunday and he wasn't expecting so many people. The train stopped at all stations and picked up more and more people as it went. At last they arrived at the station for the hospital and ninety per cent of the people got out. The hospital was out of town and people were rushing for the bus and spare taxis. The Messenger decided to walk, as he wanted them to be on their way home before he arrived.

It seemed like a very long walk to the Messenger and he thought he was getting too old for this sort of thing. Eventually he arrived and he turned into the gates. The hospital was set in woodland so he found somewhere to sit out of sight and have a rest. He settled on a grassy mound behind a tree, and opened his sports bag bringing out a flask of coffee, and a pack of sandwiches. He was in need of a cup of coffee and the sandwiches were very welcome. After twenty minutes or so he repacked his bag and carried on up the drive. As he arrived at the hospital people were leaving, as was some of the staff. Visiting hours were short here due to the severe conditions of some of the patients. He slipped around the back and went through the staff entrance, careful to avoid being seen. He peeped in the changing room. There was only one person in there and he was changing into clean overalls to do the floors after the visitors had left. It was surprising how messy the visitors were, the floors were covered with crisps, pieces of food and wrappers, discarded plastic coffee cups they had bought from the canteen earlier and muddy footprints.

When the man had gone, the Messenger slipped into the room, took a pair of fresh overalls from the pile, and went around the back behind the lockers to change. He put on Wellingtons and a mask and hat, poured some water into a bucket, then helped him self to a mop, and a plastic rubbish bag. He transferred stuff from his sports bag to the rubbish bag, and then he looked for somewhere to stash his bag and clothes. He picked on a locker that was out of sight, and gently forced the door open. It was empty so he put his stuff in there. On the inside of the door were countless porno photos,

"Pervert," said the Messenger as he eased the door shut. When he reached the private ward where Will Hargreaves was, the cleaner was there cleaning the floor. The Messenger retreated back down the hall to wait for him to leave. When he left and the Messenger watched him until he turned the corner at the other end of the corridor, to go to the next ward. He moved silently into the ward and over to the bed. Will Hargreaves eyes lit up when he saw him.

"Are you still of the same mind?" asked the Messenger.

Will blinked once.

"Is anyone due to visit you in the next half hour?"

Will blinked twice for no.

"You realise you will die before the half hour is up?"

He blinked once again.

"Is it still your wish to die?" he said gently

Will blinked once.

"Are you sure you can swallow," said the Messenger.

Will blinked once

"Then that is the first thing to do." He produced a bottle with a tube attached from his bag and gently placed the tube in Will's mouth. He held the bottle up so the fluid flowed down as you would for a baby and told Will to start sucking. It was a slow process, as Will couldn't swallow very well, but he persevered, so strong was his wish to die. When he had at last finished, the Messenger wiped his face as a little of the fluid had bubbled out.

He dived into his bag and brought out Will's Olympic medal and placed it around his neck. He had also brought the cups that Will had won in his short life. He arranged them on a trolley and pulled it close to the bed. He put Will's cycling helmet on his lap and a single tear splashed onto it. In the corner was a television and the Messenger wheeled it over to the bed and plugged into the wall. He switched it on and put in a DVD.

"It is you winning race in the Olympics in Beijing," he explained, "I thought you would like to see it one more time. There is also the bus ride you made through your home town with the other athletes."

Will blinked, and another tear ran down his face and onto his helmet. The race came onto the screen, and Will was gazing at the screen intently, tears cascading down his face. The Messenger stood close to him with his arm around the boy's shoulder, holding his hand. They watched in silence together. When the National Anthem played after he received his medal, they were both crying. They then watched his arrival home and the trip on the open topped bus through his hometown.

"Good bye dear boy," whispered the Messenger, "God bless and keep you."

Will's eyes blinked once and then fluttered shut He died with the sound of the people's cheers ringing in his ears. The Messenger wiped the tears from the boy's face and put the helmet to one side with the cups. He tucked a card under Will's hand, gathered up his bag and bucket and swiftly left.

He did not use the main drive on the way out but kept in the woods, as he came towards the main gates he could see they were locked. They were electronic gates and very tall and he knew he couldn't climb over them. They were probably alarmed anyway. He remained in the edge of the wood while he thought about it. A high fence with barbed wire surrounded the property and cameras were placed at intervals all the way around. When they found Will, and the alarm went up they would find him for sure. While he was deciding what to do the cleaner he had seen in the hospital came down the drive. He fell in quietly behind him. The cleaner swiped a card and the great heavy gates began to swing open. The Messenger rushed past the cleaner and through the gate shouting,

"Thanks-mate – Good night." There was a bus just about to go and the Messenger jumped aboard. The cleaner walked off in the other direction, and the Messenger breathed a sigh of relief. He did not want someone realising that he was not one of the staff, as least not yet. I can't keep this up he thought not at my age, especially as he was unwell himself. Only two more to go and that would be an end to it. There would be no more.

He travelled home feeling very tired. How could he have missed the fact that the gates closed at that time? He was slipping; he must take extra care next time. He thought back to Will and felt sad that the boy had suffered so much, and for so long. He had noticed the bruising and the septic looking sores on the boy's body, and he had lost most of his hair. When he held the boy's hand it had been cold and limp. Poor little sod couldn't even take a pee or scratch his nose, the only thing he could do was weep. He knew in his heart that he had done the right thing. He felt that God would forgive him, and if he didn't - the people he had helped might.

Chapter Twenty-Eight
The Discovery of Will's Death

Nurse O'Dowd walked back from her hour's break; she now had to bed down her patient Will Hargreaves for the night. She would wash him and tend his wounds and change his bags. God love him she thought, night and day were the same for him. She would give him a pain killing injection that was supposed to help him sleep, but it was no help as far as she could see, because when she checked him during the night he was always awake. She suspected that it was not strong enough, but there was no way he could tell anyone. When she looked into his eyes he seemed to be pleading for help, like a small, frightened creature caught in the headlights of a car.

That's odd she thought as she walked into the ward, he's got the television by the bed. Who did that? He couldn't do it for himself. She walked over to the bed and pushed the television to one side and realised that there was something wrong. Poor Darling she thought, he's died. "Thank-you o' merciful God," she muttered and crossed herself, and checked his pulse. She called the doctor, and he was there in seconds as he was only in the ward at the end of the hall

"Where did all this stuff come from?" demanded the doctor.

"I'm sure I don't know," said Nurse O' Dowd perhaps he's family brought it in."

"They didn't come today," said the doctor, "they called this morning and told me that they would be in tomorrow. Apparently, they had a small burglary earlier in the week and were sorting out what might be missing.

"God love him," said the nurse' "he's wearing his Olympic medal, and see here he has his cycling helmet and all his cups on the trolley."

" Let's see what he was watching on the television," said the doctor."

" That's the DVD control," said the nurse.

"Then lets see the DVD he was watching," said the doctor. They watched Will win his race and collect his gold medal. The doctor clicked off the television and pushed it back in the corner.

"I don't like this," he said, "who could have got in and set this up without being seen. I want a blood test done."

"Oh look," said Nurse O' Dowd, "He has a card under his hand."

She pulled it out and saw the name at the foot of the card – The Messenger of Death.

"Oh Lord save us, it's him," she cried. The doctor snatched the card and read it.

"Right Nurse, don't touch anything and keep everybody out. I'm going to ring the police. You remain by his side until they come." With that he left the room and ran down the corridor.

Nurse O' Dowd looked at Will's inert body and said,

"So someone helped you on your way, God knows who could blame them. You've been all but dead for a long time now. I'm sure God will forgive him, whoever he is, but it is a mortal sin to take a life." The nurse carried on talking to him as she had done when he was alive. He didn't answer then, but the nurse thought he could at least hear her, even if he couldn't answer back. People had stopped talking to him, even his visitors would only say a few words and lapse into silence, and then they would get fidgety and go home.

His mother always cried the whole time she was there, and his father said a few words and then sat in silence looking at the floor and wringing his hands.

"Well Darling," she said, "that's all over now. You've gone to a better place."

. . . .

Sunday had been a lovely day for Jean and Bland. They had gone to a pub restaurant for lunch. David and his band were playing there for the last time and the place was packed. Jean was glad that she had booked otherwise they would not have been able to get in. Seth had come to lend his support, and he and Jean and Bland had a table near the front.

"This is a lovely old medieval place," said Bland, "right on the river, lovely gardens and brightly coloured hanging baskets all around."

"The restaurant is good too," said Jean, We must come here more often. They do rooms here as well you know."

"A lovely place to spend a week-end," said Bland

"David was very good today, wasn't he?"

"Yes," said Bland, "he deserves his chance in America."

Later in the day, as it was such a lovely warm afternoon they had tea in the garden. Bland liked the concept of English afternoon tea, it was so civilised, and Jean's teas were the best.

Bland's mobile phone suddenly rang.

"Sorry," he said getting up and moving away from the table to answer it.

"Bland," he said, "Oh hello Boyd – where are you now? – Well stay there and I'll come to you. It should take me about half an hour – have we been officially asked to take over? - Right see you later." He put his phone away.

"Sorry folks I've got to go, the Messenger has struck again. This time it's outside London. It's that young cyclist Will Hargreaves, the gold medallist who was struck by that lorry and paralysed. See you all later in the week. He kissed Jean on the cheek and went into the house to collect his briefcase and coat and set off for the hospital.

Chapter Twenty-Nine
At The Hospital

An hour later he arrived and Boyd was waiting for him.

"Sorry I'm late Boyd but the traffic was a little heavier than anticipated."

As they walked along the corridor to the ward Boyd said,

"This was welled plannned Sir. The security gates are only open for a short time on a Sunday, about an hour to let the visitors in and out. He must have done it after visiting hour, that's when most of the staff go home. They have one cleaner who comes in at the end of visiting, he cleans the floors and collects the rubbish and then he goes home. He only does this part of the building. There are only six wards with one person in each."

"Did he do this one?" said Bland

"Yes Sir. This is his first ward, he always starts here."

"So the Messenger must have come in after he had gone."

"Yes Sir," said Boyd, "but here is the interesting part, the cleaner has a swipe card for the electronic gate, as it is always closed when he leaves. Today however, as the gate swung open someone overtook him and shouted good-night and ran to catch the bus."

"Did he see who it was?"

"No Sir, he only saw him from behind. He was wearing a track suit with the hood up and carrying a sports bag so he thought it was a physiotherapist."

"Is that possible Boyd?"

"No Sir, they don't come in at week-ends." They walked over to the bed and looked down at Will.

"Poor little sod," said Bland

"I guess that's why the Messenger picked him Sir. He had been to Will's parents house in the week, and stolen the cups and Will's Olympic medal, and the helmet he was wearing on his winning race. He must have died watching himself winning the race in Beijing on the DVD. Here's the card he left."

"Read it out Boyd,"

"Yes Sir,

Will Hargreaves our cycling hero tall and strong
Looked forward to a life that was happy and long
Brought back Olympic Gold from Beijing's fair city
He was to marry his sweetheart who was clever and pretty

Hurtling down the road, one early misty morning
Doing his training while other were still yawning
Over the hill came a fast juggernaut speeding
The man at the wheel was tired and dreaming

Too late the driver saw him and tried to turn aside
At the bend in the road, they were forced to collide
The driver jumped down and ran back to find
Will's body twisted and still, on the road behind.

Will awoke in hospital; he would never be the same
Gone was his previous life, and gone was his fame.
Now he was a vegetable and he could not complain
He'd be forever silent, still, and doomed to rigid pain.

Trapped in a body that was full of pain and sorrow
Paralysed today, and the same fate tomorrow
Unable to speak, or even lift a finger
Left to rot in silent pain, and left to forever linger

He prayed for release from his accused empty life
He would never have children, and never have a wife.
The Messenger came to help him, pitying him in his plight
He would release him from his savage pain and lead him to the
    light

He died watching his race once more and hearing the cheers
Wild acclaim from the people ringing in his ears
Watching the triumph as he collected his medal on screen
He closed his eyes for the last time on this happy scene.

The Messenger of Death

It's the usual on the back Sir, date of birth, name and address, and date
of death."

"He excelled himself this time Boyd, seven verses, it's a wonder he could
find a card big enough, his poetry lacks a certain something."

"The writing is very small Sir."

"It would need to be Boyd."

"The doctor said that he died some time after four o' clock, that ties in with the nurse who had her break from four until five. The cleaner also works from four until five so the Messenger must have followed him in. He cut it fine Sir because the electronic gate was closed when he left. If the cleaner hadn't have left at that time he would have been trapped in the grounds."

"A careless mistake Boyd, he didn't check on the gates." The forensic people were hovering, waiting to get on, so Bland and Boyd left them to it.

"Have you interviewed everyone Boyd?"

"Yes Sir, the doctor, Nurse O' Dowd, the cleaner, the people on reception. There are only two on reception on Sundays, and they cover each other for breaks. They both swear that nobody came in that they didn't know, and all visitors had to sign in and sign out again."

"Cameras?"

"None Sir, except on the perimeter wall, and they don't come on until seven at night and go off at six o' clock the following morning."

"Well Boyd you've done an excellent job here, we'll speak to the doctor and then go home. There's nothing more we can do here."

"The doctor's office is down the next corridor Sir." When they arrived at the doctor's office he was not in a happy mood. He had just rung the parents and they wanted to collect their son's body, and he had to explain that they couldn't have it, as there had to be an autopsy to find the cause or causes of death.

"Did they seem surprised at his death?" asked Bland.

"No, they insist it was natural causes. The autopsy will soon show what the causes were, although the situation he was found in points to the fact that someone saw fit to end it for him. The card tells you that."

"Well doctor we are going back to London now. We will arrange to see the parents, but not today, good bye and thank you so much for your cooperation."

"Not much choice have I?" said the doctor and he swept out of the office.

"Time to go Boyd."

"Yes Sir."

Later back at the office Bland reminded Boyd to wear a dark suit and a tie on Monday, for the funeral. Although they would not be by the graveside as mourners they would be near by. They were to observe, they would see who attended and who came to watch at a distance.

"We'll fit the parents in sometime in the afternoon," said Bland.

"Mrs Bland still in Haversham Sir?"

"Yes Boyd,"

"I guess she'll miss David and Seth when they go to America."

"Yes," said Bland, "that is why I left her behind in Haversham. She'll come back later in the week and bring the boys with her, and they will stay with us until they go to America."

"Amanda is visiting her mother this week."

"Well Boyd, you know what that means."

"No Sir,"

"It means that I will buy you a pint on the way home."

"Thank-you Sir, usual place Sir?"

"Where else Boyd, where else indeed."

Chapter Thirty
Willie's Funeral

The funeral was due to start at eleven o' clock and Bland and Boyd were already there standing under some trees by a large tomb, virtually out of sight.

There did not seem to be anyone else about and the place was eerily quiet.

"Bit of a difference to the last funeral we attended Sir," whispered Boyd.

"I'll say," said Bland quietly, "and no tomatoes thank God."

"No Sir," said Boyd.

Several people walked along the path, but they were here to tend graves and put fresh flowers in pots. Bland watched them all

Presently the funeral party arrived and went into the church. It was a very poor affair, affair half an hour they came out of the church and moved to the graveside. The coffin was lowered and the parson said his piece. Apart from Willie's brother, only two other people turned up. One was the doctor from Guys and the other was the landlord from the Travellers Rest where Willie's body was found. The landlord's wife refused to attend. Oddly enough, thought the landlord, the fact that Willie had been found in his pub had been good for business. Everybody wanted to see where the body was found, and to sit in the chair; it seemed to give them some kind of ghoulish pleasure. Weird, some folk.

Bland scanned the horizon, looking for any moment in the trees, or around the graves, but he could see nothing.

"See anything Boyd?" he said.

"No Sir." The funeral party moved off, they all shook hands with the vicar and went their separate ways.

"Well Sir, that was a waste of time,"

"Seems so Boyd, lets take a look at the floral tributes." They walked slowly down to the grave and looked at the flowers. There was a wreath from his brother, one from the doctor and a bunch of flowers from the publican. There was also one more very pretty wreath, with the message:

Good-bye old friend – sorry I could not attend
They are watching.

"Damn," exploded Bland. There was nothing on the wreath to say which flower shop it had been purchased. They would not be able to trace it

"Take a picture of it Boyd."

"Yes Sir."

"This is beautifully made," said Bland, "But there is something about it, I just cant put my finger on it."

"Better get back Sir, we have Will Hargreaves parents coming in at two o' clock."

"Right Boyd we'll pick up a sandwich on the way back to the office."

AS they drove back to the office Bland wondered what it was that was bubbling about in the back of his head. What was it that he knew but couldn't recall? Suddenly he said,

"Boyd drive to the hotel that the brother is staying at, and make haste, he may have already gone back to Scotland,"

"When they arrived at the hotel they had got there just in time. He was at the reception desk, with his case, paying his bill.

"Mr Johnson, I'm Detective Chief Inspector Bland, we spoke when you arrived to identify your brothers body."

"Ah yes Inspector, what can I do for you?"

"Your brother told the doctor that he was staying with an old friend, someone that he had known for years. Have you any idea who that might be?"

"Not at all Inspector, we didn't keep in touch, even when we were young we didn't move in the same circle of friends."

"And the wreath Sir, the extra wreath?"

"Strange that," said Mr Johnson, "the undertaker said that they went to the chapel of rest to collect the body and placed the coffin in the hearse and laid my wreath on top. They returned to the chapel to collect the doctor's wreath and lock up, and when they got back to the hearse there it was on top of the coffin, next to mine. Do you suspect it was the killer."

"Oh yes indeed Sir, I'm sure of it."

"Well good luck to you in finding him Inspector. I'm away back home now," he said picking up his case, "my taxi for the station has just arrived, Good day to you both," he strode out of the hotel and jumped into his taxi and was off. Bland stared after him,

"He neither knows nor cares," said Bland.

"Yes Sir," said Boyd, "we better get a move on."

"Indeed," said Bland looking at his watch. They picked up sandwiches and coffee on the way back and had lunch at their desks.

Chapter Thirty-One
Will's Parents

Will's parents were a little late as they got held up in the traffic. Constable Grey escorted them to Bland's office. Bland jumped up to greet them,

"I'm Detective Chief Inspector Bland and this is my Sergeant Darren Boyd, please take a seat." When they were settled he asked them if they would care for some tea, and the both said yes.

"I must apologise for making you come here instead of travelling to you, but the Sergeant and I had to go to a funeral this morning."

"That's all right," said Mr Hargreaves, "we understand. It was that tramp, wasn't it?"

"Yes indeed."

"Poor man," said Mr Hargreaves. Mrs Hargreaves, who had not spoken up until now, suddenly burst out,

"No he wasn't poor, he was lucky, as our son was lucky, Will is now free. FREE, FREE, FREE," she shouted at the top of her voice.

"Maureen dear," said her husband putting his arm around her and patting her hand. She was now in floods of tears. Not the silent ones that ran down her face when she sat in the hospital with her son, but noisy sobbing, the kind that was a release of pent up misery and emotions. A sudden release of grief.

Constable Grey came in with the tea and Bland noticed that he had managed to scrounge a few biscuits from somewhere.

Thank-you Constable, thank-you very much indeed," he said as the constable hastened from the room. Crying women was not his scene.

Bland got up and opened the cupboard behind him and brought out a bottle of brandy.

"Would you care for a small drop in your tea? Purely for medicinal purposes of course," he said.

"A large drop would be better," said Mr Hargreaves.

"Me too," said Mrs Hargreaves through her sobs, "a very large drop."

The biscuits were handed around and Bland could feel Boyd's disapproval – plying witnesses with drink- it wasn't right. He looked at Boyd and could see him frowning

" Now Mr and Mrs Hargreaves, "tell us anything you can," said Boyd getting out his pad and licking his pencil.

"Like what?" said Mr Hargreaves holding his cup up for more brandy, and Mrs Hargreaves did likewise.

"Whether he had any visitors that you weren't aware of?"

"There was no one," said Mrs Hargreaves, pulling herself together now, and if someone came and visited him, when the staff was otherwise occupied, how would we know? Will couldn't tell us. You know when he first had the accident I prayed for him to live, and when he did and I saw the kind of life he had ahead of him, I prayed for him to die. I would have done it myself if I had been able to. I hope whoever did it never gets caught. He gave our beloved son a decent death, surrounded by all his achievements, and for that I thank him." She sat there looking defiant and held her cup up for more brandy, and Mr Hargreaves held his up too. Bland gave them a large measure and he could hear Boyd's snort of disapproval in the background. He looked at his nearly empty bottle, and sighed, and put it back in the cupboard.

"You mustn't mind my wife Inspector, she been very distraught of late," said Mr Hargreaves.

"We understand," said Bland kindly.

"So there's nothing unusual that you can think of," continued Boyd.

"No Sergeant," said Mr Hargreaves.

"Well Mr and Mrs Hargreaves it was most kind of you to come in and see us," said Bland, "how are you getting home?"

"A taxi to the station and then a train home. We only live five minutes from the station."

"Then we will get a car to take you to the station," said Bland, "could you see to that Sergeant?"

"Yes Sir," said Boyd and left the room.

"Inspector, would you come to my son's funeral?"

"I would be honoured," said Bland.

"And your Sergeant of course."

"Thank-you," said Bland.

"When can we have his body?"

"I'm not sure," said Bland, "there will have to be an autopsy."

"Why an autopsy?" said Mrs Hargreaves.

"There was no doctor present at his death and in view of the circumstances in which he died, foul play is suspected, so there has to be an autopsy. An inquest will probably follow almost immediately and I feel sure the body will be released then. I'm sorry if this seems a waste of time to you but be have to explore every avenue, we can't have people acting a though they are God."

"Why not," said Mrs Hargreaves, "I for one will be forever grateful."

"Well," said Bland patiently, "no one has the right to say who is to live and who is to die. Only the person concerned has that right, and at the present moment in time, even they don't have the right to say when they want to go.

Until that time comes when they do have the right, we have to uphold the law, that is what we are paid for. What would happen if the Messenger sent someone on their way who did not want to go?"

"I hear what you are saying Inspector, and I understand your situation but please don't try too hard to find him." Boyd popped his head around the door.

"Car's ready Sir," he said.

"Well thank-you again for coming, and have a safe journey home" said Bland rising to shake hands with them. Mrs Hargreaves found that the brandy had gone to her legs and Mr Hargreaves had to steer her out of the office.

"See you at the funeral Inspector, and you too Sergeant," he called out as he went through the door. Constable Grey had come to escort them to the car. As they got seated in the back of the car Constable Grey leaned in the window to wish them good bye and was assailed by the brandy fumes coming up to greet him. God, he thought, they stink of drink. That's a bloody disgrace, especially as their son has only just died, some people he thought as the car pulled away into the traffic.

Back in the office Bland told Boyd that they had been invited to Will's funeral.

"That's quite useful," said Bland, "there will be a lot of people there and the Messenger will feel safer and perhaps wont be so careful about hiding himself. We may stand a chance

Chapter Thirty-Two
Lenny's Visit And A Look At The Galleries

Tuesday morning and Bland was just having his breakfast when he got a call form Andrew Middleton

"Robert," he said "could you and you Sergeant pop in and see me today?"

"Is it about –" here he was interrupted.

"It's about that little matter we discussed last week, come up for lunch. See you about one o' clock. Bye for now." The phone went dead.

Well, thought Bland, perhaps he found out too much and is being extra careful.

When Boyd came to pick him up he told him about the call.

"Well if it's a free lunch Sir, that cant be bad."

"Really Boyd, "my feeling is that he has found out something very delicate that can't be talked about over the phone."

"Or maybe he's found out nothing at all and lunch is a compensation." When they reached the office Lenny the Dip was waiting for them.

"Not him again," said Bland exasperatedly

"Shall I tell him to push off Sir?"

"No, bring him along to the office."

"Well what is it this time Lenny?" said Bland, hanging up his jacket and flopping down in his swing chair.

"Got some information for you that might be worth something," said Lenny slyly.

"About what?" said Boyd.

"About the death of Louis Gordino," said Lenny, pleased with himself.

"Then you'd better tell Detective Atkins, it's his case not mine," said Bland

"Don't want to," said Lenny sullenly.

"Why not?" said Boyd.

"He kicked me down the steps last time I saw 'im." Bland smiled, he remembered it well, Lenny had tied to extract money from Dave Atkins for information that the detective already knew and he tried to insist the he should be paid as it wasn't his fault that the detective already had the information. Dave Atkins was not known for his patience and when Lenny would not take no for an answer he kicked him down the steps. Dave was reprimanded by the Super but didn't care because he had the satisfaction . Lenny decided to bring a charge against him, but the Super told Lenny that they were thinking of bringing charges against him for wasting police time and trying to extract money under false pretences, and furthermore if he didn't leave the police premises at once the Super himself would take great pleasure in also kicking him down the steps.

"Well Lenny, what's the information?"

"Just before he died Louis Gordino visited the Hugget brothers." Bland picked up the phone and called his colleague,

"Dave, Robert here, I've got Lenny the Dip in the office with me, he's trying to shake me down for some money, he reckons that Louis Gordino visited the Hugget brothers on the morning of his death." There was a short silence and then he said,

"Really, well done. Yes, the odious little creep is with me at the moment – I'll tell him. Thanks – see you later."

"It would seem that Detective Atkins already knew that Louis Gordino visited the Hugget brothers and Big Harry the day of his death. He has statements to that effect. It seems that he arrested Tomasino Codova in the early hours of this morning and he has confessed. He was the hit man for Myra Cambora, as everybody but you suspected. He also said that I'm not to give you a brass farthing. See him off the premises Sergeant."

"It will be a pleasure Sir," said Boyd. When Boyd and Lenny left the room he turned his attention to the files on his desk. The autopsy on Will Hargreaves showed he had been poisoned. No news there thought Bland. Boyd returned,

"I almost kicked him down the steps myself Sir, I can't stand that little toe rag. Beats me why you put up with him."

"I have my reasons Boyd, Will was poisoned, he had taken it by mouth through a tube, it must have been difficult for him."

"It shows his determination to die Sir."

"Indeed," aid Bland, "Boyd I think we'll visit the Hugget brothers before we go up west for lunch."

"Going to warn them about Lenny Sir,"

"Certainly not Boyd, that would be most unprofessional."

"Right Sir."

"No, I thought we'd take a look at the new show area and see what they've done with Jean's dresses."

"Very well Sir."

When they arrived, the Galleries were a hive of activity. Quentin was beside himself, rushing about all over the place.

"I think we'll visit Steve first Boyd, less manic."

"Yes Sir, I see Quentin has got the wind under his tail."

They went into the studio and Steve was sitting in the corner in his wheelchair painting orchids. A large pot was on a stand in front of him.

"Morning Steve."

"Morning Mr Bland Sir, morning Sergeant."

"How are you?"

"Oh bearing up Mr Bland Sir."

"You're not working too hard are you?"

"Oh no Sir."

"Well I think you're looking very tired. Tell you what I'll make us all a drink. Go and tell the others Boyd, they're roaring about like maniacs at the moment. Steve and Bland went into the kitchen and Bland made coffee and everybody came to sit for five minutes and have a well-deserved break.

"Queenie," said Bland, "I think Steve is looking very tired and that arm doesn't look good, its seems very swollen, look at his fingers."

"I'm alright really Mr Bland, the arm 'as always been a bit painful."

"No you're not alright," said Bland, "you weren't brought over to this side of the river to work yourself to death." Queenie peered at him,

"You look 'orrible, I'm calling the doctor right now," she said, we've all been so busy that we aven't been taking proper attention, it's a good job you came in Mr. Bland."

"Boyd and I came in to see how the new dress shop is coming along."

"Oh it's a treat," said Queenie.

"It's a salon for gowns," said Quentin, "and its not nearly ready yet," he said getting into another flap.

"Well lets go and look anyway," said Bland, now that we've finished our coffee." They went through to the gown section.

"Well," said Bland, "I step back in amazement, this is truly magnificent." The gowns were on models on raised pedestals so that you could walk around them and view from all angles. They were beautifully lit and the silks and satins shimmered in the light, and the sequins and beads twinkled like a thousand small stars.

"Its better than the west end," said Boyd, "wait until Amanda sees this."

Someone had come in through the warehouse door at the back and called out. Teddy went to see who it was. He came back a moment later with Frenchie and Florentine. Many years ago when they were young in Paris they had fallen in love. It was just after the Second World War. However Florentine's father had insisted that she marry another man chosen by him. He was a rich businessman, who would look after her. Florentine being the dutiful daughter complied with her father's wishes and a broken hearted Frenchie came to London to seek his fortune. He never returned to Paris and he never married, there was no one for him but Florentine. Although she was married to Auguste for many years, when he died she felt relief, not grief. Their marriage had been a polite association, no joy and no laughter. Auguste was not interested in the physical side of marriage and they had separate rooms. She suspected that he was gay, she had heard rumours the he was a regular visitor to a young man in the Latin Quarter. Their marriage was a façade, something to keep the polite society in which they moved happy. They did nothing to upset the boat of respectability.

Several months after Auguste's death Florentine decided to go to London and look for Frenchie, she wanted to find out what had happened to him. At their first meeting they realised that their love for each other was as strong as it ever was, and the decided to spend the rest of their lives together.

"Bonjour mon chere amis," he said, "Florentine and I 'ave come to invite you to our wedding in two weeks time. It is just a small private affair. Florentine has now resided in the parish for the required amount of time, so it will be at the local church, at three o' clock on Sunday the twenty-sixth. We are only inviting you Teddy and Arthur and Queenie and Quentin. We would also like to invite Mr Bland, and his lovely wife, and Sergeant Boyd and his very pretty girlfriend. We will have ze wedding breakfast, or tea, or what ever you English call it, at our place above the shop. We both hope that you will all come, it would make us very 'appy. No presents by request we already 'ave everything we need" Everybody gave their congratulations and promised to be there.

"Now," said Frenchie, we 'ave some zing for you." And he placed the large cardboard book he was carrying on the table. He lifted the lid and gently drew back the tissue revealing a beautiful French doll. It was about two and a half feet high and dressed in the style of Marie Antoinette. The last time Bland had seen the doll, it had been in a state of disrepair, on a shelf in Frenchie's shop. The dress and the lace had been torn and was hanging down. The tall wig had been dirty and matted and was covered in dirty flowers and flies and one of the shoes was missing. Now it was exquisite, the old silk and lace had been cleaned and repaired, some of the skirt, had been tastefully replaced by Florentine. The tall white wig had been cleaned and built up again with every hair in place, and small silk flowers adorned it. The petticoats had benefited from a good but gentle clean and Frenchie had made her new shoes.

"We thought you could use 'er to advertise your business, maybe on ze counter."

"Counter nothing," said Quentin, "this gorgeous creature is going right at the front of the window where all can see her." He set her up on her own pedestal and made everyone go outside to see if she looked right, which of course she did, everybody gave the thumbs up sign, and trooped back inside again.

"Like the flowers around the bay window Teddy."

"Thank-you Mr Bland, they is from our allotment."

"Better than that false grass that everybody is using these days," said Bland, "why only this morning some false grass was brought into the office and I didn't like it at all." Bland stared meaningfully at Teddy. Teddy stared back and after a moment said, "Did you not Mr Bland?" What the hell is he talking about thought Boyd; we didn't have any false grass in the office this morning. He's losing the plot.

"You'll have to watch out for pickpockets on Saturday Teddy. All those people at your opening, it's bound to attract them. Nobody wants someone dipping into their pockets."

"No," said Teddy, "me and Arfer will be looking out for dips – one well known dip in particular."

"Knew you would," said Bland, "now we must be off, we are having lunch with an old friend at one o' clock. Say good-bye to the others for us and let me know about Steve."

"Will do Mr Bland, thanks for popping in, got your meaning," he said touching the side of his nose, "see you Saturday."

"Looking forward to it," said Bland, "come along Boyd, standing there with your mouth open, you look like the village idiot."

Chapter Thirty-Three
Andrew and the Black Book

When they arrived at Andrew's office he was waiting outside. He jumped into the car and directed them to the restaurant. They parked and went into the restaurant; Andrew led them through the restaurant, through the kitchen and out into the back alley. They crossed the yard and went into the kitchen of another restaurant opposite, they walked through into the dining room, and were directed to a private booth. They were given menus and the drinks order was taken and the waiter left closing the curtain behind him.

"Do I detect a touch of the secret squirrel?" said Bland.

"Just being cautious Robert," said Andrew. Boyd was completely out of his depth. He began to suspect that the older members of the police force and it seemed the security forces were losing their marbles. Andrew had a small document case with him, which he pushed across to Bland.

"Your will find the book in there, together with reports and photographs. You were right, as always, it was who you thought it was. My advice to you is to put it in a safe place, and pursue it no further. If it got back to the person concerned that this information was out, many lives would be forfeited, yours and mine included. Having said my piece let's now enjoy our lunch. Bland

149

slipped the case under the table down by his feet, out of sight. The curtain was pulled back and the waiter was standing there with their drinks.

"Leave the curtain back now please," said Andrew.

"Yes Sir," said the waiter, he took their order and said,

"Luigi will bring your lunch as soon as it is ready."

"Thank-you," said Andrew, "we are in no rush."

"Now," he said turning to Bland, "tell me more about the Huggets and their new endeavour, are you going to the opening?"

"I'll say," said Bland, "Jean would never forgive me if we didn't."

"What about you Boyd?" said Andrew.

"I'm going," said Boyd, "my girlfriend says so." Andrew laughed heartily. They chatted about this and that, and before they knew it the waiter arrived with a trolley and lunch was served. As it was an Italian restaurant they had gone for a selection of pasta dishes. The table was soon covered with food so they could help themselves and sample all the dishes. There were two jugs of water lots of garlic bread and red wine.

"Just one glass for you Boyd, you're driving," said Bland.

"Yes Sir," said Boyd, he was not too disappointed because he was more of a beer man himself.

While they were eating Bland and Andrew were talking about old times of which Boyd knew nothing, so he busied himself with his food and people watching as they went past the window. One man looked in and then went on past, then came back from the opposite direction, and looked in again. He pretended to read the menu in the window, but he seemed to be watching them.

Boyd nudged Bland,

"Don't look now," he said quietly, "but I think we are being spied on, He's walked past the window twice and now he's pretending to read the menu." Andrew glanced carefully over his shoulder and muttered 'damn' quietly under his breath,

"We've been followed."

"Do you know him?" asked Bland.

"Yes," said Andrew, "he's one of the nastier elements of the security forces."

"He's coming in," said Bland, "invite him over Andrew, you know what they say, keep your friends close, but keep your enemies closer. If he wants to know what we are talking about, let him. We'll bore him to death in five minutes." Andrew waved him over; the man came over unsure of what was going on. Andrew got up and greeted him enthusiastically.

"Sergio," he said shaking him warmly by the hand, "what are you doing in this part of town – you've found out my secret haven't you – this wonderful Italian restaurant. Join us." The man hesitated, this was not what he expected.

"Come now I won't take no for an answer, everybody has to eat. You're not with anyone, are you?" he said looking around; he knew they always worked in pairs. If Sergio was with anyone he certainly was not going to tell Andrew. Andrew signalled the waiter, who came straight away.

"Drinks for my friend, and some more dishes please, and more garlic bread." The waiter hurried away.

"Now," said Andrew let me introduce you to everyone. Sergio this is Detective Chief Inspector Robert Bland and his Sergeant Darren Boyd, and gentlemen this is Sergio Casparin from the security services. Now lets have some more wine and tuck in." Boyd thought he might get a second glass of wine but Band moved quickly and filled Boyd's glass water. Never takes his eye of the ball, thought Boyd, crafty old bugger. Bland and Andrew chatted away to Sergio, telling him how they met many years ago, and every once in a while they would meet up for a meal when circumstances allowed. Boyd tucked into his food again and watched the passers by.

Presently there was another man walking past the window and looking in. He also pretended to read the menu. Andrew had also seen him it was just what he was waiting for, he knew there would be another one. The man outside was dithering, not sure whether to come in to the restaurant.

"Well bless my soul," said Andrew in mock surprise "isn't that Boris Rasputin outside? What a coincidence." He jumped up and rushed over to the door, whipping it open and dragging the man in, slapping him on the back like a long lost friend. Andrew made everyone move up and sat him down. The waiter arrived at that moment bearing more dishes and wine and a mountain of garlic bread.

"Isn't this splendid," said Andrew, "this is Boris Rasputin, he used to work with Sergio when they first came out of Russia Ex KGB aren't you?" They both denied it profusely.

"Oh well," said Andrew, "it was such a long time ago, one forgets." He dished up plates of pasta for his two new guests, gave them a pile of garlic bread and filled their glasses to the brim with wine.

"Come along," he said, eat drink and be merry for tomorrow we die, as the saying goes. Tell us what are you doing these days?" They all looked expectantly at the Russians

"I am doin nozzing at ze moment," said Sergio, in a thick accent.

"I am doin nozzing also," said Boris drinking his wine.

"Are you doing nozzing together?" asked Andrew.

"We are not togezzer," said Sergio.

"No," echoed Boris. Liars thought Andrew.

"What no spies to chase, no secrets to find?" said Andrew refilling their glasses. The Russians felt distinctly uncomfortable, they had been instructed to follow Andrew, but to keep a low profile, he was not to know that he was being followed, and here they were wining and dining with him. This would not go down well at headquarters, but the wine was taking effect and they were beginning not to care.

"We haf many important zings we haf to do," said Sergio, "but we not talk about zat."

"Oh hush, hush stuff," said Andrew nodding his head and pouring more wine, "enough said old boy, and we'll say no more." There was a few moments silence and then Andrew said,

"Robert and his Sergeant are working on the Messenger of Death case at the moment."

"You no find the murderer yet," said Sergio, "is not good, maybe you haf many more murders."

"No we haven't found him yet but we will, we believe he will kill again, but not too many times we trust," said Bland. They all chatted on for about a half an hour or so, but it was very guarded and awkward. The Russians were well into the wine now but Bland and Andrew and Boyd were only drinking water now,

"Let's have some delicious ice cream," said Andrew, and the menus were brought and the ice cream was ordered. Both Sergio and Boris loved ice cream; it was the thing they liked most about the west.

"We must have a sweet wine to go with them," said Andrew.

"Oh no, no," said the Russians.

"Just one little glass," said Andrew, "how can that make a difference?"

"Oh just ze one," said Sergio, and he giggled, "just ze one leetle glass."

"Good," said Andrew, "I'll get them myself". He got up and went to the bar; presently he came back with five glasses on a tray.

"Here we are," he said putting the tray down, "five nice glasses of champagne. See how well it goes down with ice cream."

Champagne – the Russians gulped it down – when did they ever get champagne. Boyd was rather pleased to get a glass of champagne. When they had finished their sweets, it was decided to sit in the bar area, in deep leather armchairs and to have brandy and coffee.

Andrew and Bland guided them to their seats, in the far corner, almost out of sight. Andrew started to order but Bland said,

"Just coffee for us Andrew, we have to be getting back."

"I have to go now," said Andrew, "I'll settle the bill and leave quietly, hopefully they won't notice. You have your coffee and keep chatting to them. Mickey Finn will do the rest.

"You didn't?" said Bland.

"I did," said Andrew, "in the champagne glasses. Lets hope that that right ones got the right glasses," he smiled and slipped away.

Bland and Boyd finished their coffee and as they got up to leave two burly waiters appeared. The Russians were snoring.

"Your car has been brought around Sir and it's in the alley at the back. Every thing is taken care of; we will look after the Russian gentlemen."

"Thank-you," said Bland, and he and Boyd got up and left. The waiters cleared away the cups and glasses and left the sleeping beauties to wake up in their own good time, which was the plan.

Chapter Thirty-Four
Back at the Office

When Andrew got back to the office, his door was standing open and his secretary was standing there with her arms folded, and a very annoyed expression on her face. As he went in two burly men were looking through his ancient filing cabinet and desk.

"What the devil is going on here?" he demanded.

"Sorry Sir," said one of the men, "we have our orders."

"Who from?"

"We're not at liberty to say Sir, where's your computer."

"I don't have one."

"What about your reports."

"My secretary does them on her computer, in her office, at the other end of the corridor."

"Right Sir, then we'll go and look there."

"I don't think so," said Andrew, "nobody is allowed to see our files as they are security sensitive. You have to have special clearance. Wait until I've spoken to Colonel Forster." He rang Forster and told him the situation, but Forster did not seem to know what was going on, or at least he professed not too.

"Got nothing sensitive on the computer have you Andrew?"

"Certainly not Sir."

"Well let the blighters have a look there's a good chap, and then perhaps we can get them out of the building and out of our hair."

"Very well Sir, but it doesn't sit well with me."

"Good man," said Forster and put the phone down.

"You may take a look at it," said Andrew.

"We'll have to take it away, " said the man, "and all the files from the cabinet."

"Then I want a receipt, and when the files come back I want them in the exact order in which you found them."

"Yes Sir," said the man, and he told the other man to collect everything up and make it quick.

"The reports that Andrew had given Bland had not been done on the computer, but on an old sit up and beg ancient typewriter. It was a museum piece and lived on the floor in the corner of his secretary's office. No notes were kept and no copies were made, the typewriter ribbon was always destroyed after use, and his secretary took the shredded notes and the ribbon down to the small furnace, in the basement and watched until everything was completely burned.

Andrews leather work file had thick cardboard pages, each page was of a different colour. If Andrew put his notes behind the blue page then his secretary new exactly what to do. They would find no trace of anything to do with the black book.

"Well," said Andrew to his secretary, "we can't work so we might as well go home. I'll see you tomorrow."

"Good-night Mr Middleton," she said, "I might take this opportunity to do a little shopping. See you tomorrow." They both left the building and went their separate ways.

. . . .

On their way back to the office Boyd asked Bland what was going on.

"I think it's all to do with the black book Boyd we seemed to have stirred up a hornets nest. I'll read the reports tonight and let you know tomorrow."

"Those Russians know how to drink Sir."

"They certainly do, specially when the drink's free. They were following Andrew, there is no doubt about that, and now they have to explain how they finished up dining with him, getting drunk and passing out. I think heads are going to roll – just a moment Boyd, where are we going?"

"The hospital Sir, you have a four thirty appointment."

"Oh forget that Boyd."

"No Sir, I can see that you are suffering with your arm at the moment. The old wound must be infected, what does Mrs Bland say?"

"Nothing Boyd, I always keep it covered and anyway she's not there to see it at the present moment,"

"I'll tell her."

"You wouldn't."

"I would."

"That's blackmail."

"Yes it is Sir, so what is it to be? We go to the hospital now, or you suffer Mrs Bland's wrath later."

"Oh well," said Bland resigned, "it's rude not to turn up for an appointment, especially a doctor."

"Of course it is Sir," said Boyd, as he swung the car into the hospital car park. Bland was muttering away about being blackmailed by his own sergeant,

"I never did in all my life," he said.

"Come now Sir," said Boyd as he slid into a parking space, "you must have done – got any change?"

"Change!" said Bland, "it's outrageous, having to pay in a hospital car park."

"I know Sir I'm always saying it." Boyd helped himself to one two pound coin and two one pound coins out of Bland's hand.

"Pure extortion," said Bland, Boyd agreed and went off to get a ticket.

Left alone Bland had to admit that the old bullet wound had flared up and was weeping, if Jean saw it there would be hell to pay. Boyd suddenly popped up in front of him.

"Got another pound Sir – the prices went up this morning."

"I don't want to buy the car park Boyd, I only want the use of a small space for an hour or so."

"I know that Sir but it's still a pound. Pay up and smile."

Bland paid up but he did not smile.

Chapter Thirty-Five
Steve

Meanwhile in another part of the hospital Teddy and Arthur were sitting outside the doctor's office waiting for Steve

"Nice of Mr Bland to drop in this morning," said Arthur

"Yes," said Teddy, "and the information was useful."

"What information?"

"Seems Lenny the Dip has been grassing us up to Mr Bland."

"Really," said Arthur, "I didn't 'ear 'im say that."

"Well 'e didn't say it right owt, Arfer 'e is a man of discretion, but I knew what 'e meant."

"We'd better keep an eye on the crafty little bleeder," said Arthur.

"He's bound to turn up on Saturday," said Teddy, "trying to dip a few pockets."

"Shall we warn 'im off Teddy?"

"Nah," said Teddy, "I think Big 'Arry is the one to 'ave a word wiv 'im."

The surgery door opened and the doctor came out pushing Steve in his wheelchair.

"Ah Mr Hugget," he said, "we are going to keep Steve in, just for a couple of days. I think a small operation on that arm might make life a lot easier for him. He's worried that he might not be at the Galleries for the opening but I have assured him that he will be there. The surgeon can fit him in, and will operate on him first thing tomorrow and he should be out by Friday. If he doesn't have it tomorrow, he will have to wait another six weeks before the surgeon in available again."

Right," said Teddy, "you 'ave this done Steve. Quentin will see all is well in the Gallery, you know you can trust 'im. We will visit you and bring you 'ome when the doctor says its okay. If you don't do this you will 'ave Queenie to reckon with. Me and Arfer will go home and get your bits and pieces and be back later." Steve agreed and a porter came to collect him, and take him to the ward. When he was gone the doctor reminded them to bring in his medicine.

"He needs a rest," he said, "a really good rest with plenty of good food. It's obvious that he's not eating properly."

"Right," said Teddy, "we'll see what we can arrange. Thanks doctor."

"Your welcome," said the doctor and he disappeared back into his surgery.

When they got back and told Queenie, she took over. She went up to Steve's flat and declared that although Steve's clothes were clean they were very threadbare and on their last legs. Everything would have to be replaced. She put on her outdoor coat and hat, grabbed her purse, and called a taxi. By the time it arrived she had made a long list, case, pyjamas, dressing gown, slippers, underwear, clothes to come home in, a decent coat, toiletries and so the list went on.

"Well," said Teddy as he and Arthur watched the taxi disappear up the road, "that's Steve sorted. We 'ad better go and give Quentin a 'and before 'e throws a wobbler."

"Can't we 'ide up the allotment," suggested Arthur.

"No we can't," said Teddy, There is a time for 'iding up the allotment and this is not one of them."

Teddy phoned Big Harry to tell him about Lenny, and Big Harry promised to phone back later and let them know what he was going to arrange. He said to tell little Arthur not to worry.

"'E ain't going to bump 'im off is 'e?" said Arthur.

"Don't be daft Bruv 'e's just going to let 'im see the error of 'is ways."

Chapter Thirty-Six
Andrew Middleton

When Andrew got home that evening, he realised that his apartment had been thoroughly searched. Very carefully done but he knew that they had been there. The telephone was bugged and a couple of small cameras had been installed. There were two listening bugs in his sitting room and one in the bedroom.

Andrew only used the apartment to sleep in, as he usually went home to his estate in the country at the weekends. He never entertained at home preferring to take his guests to a good restaurant. He never brought work home so there was nothing to find. He left everything where it was and phoned his housekeeper to see if they had moved onto the estate.

"Hello Sir," she said.

"Won't be home this weekend Mrs Mannering, I'm going to the opening of the Galleries, might be able to pick up a couple of cabinets for you, one for the silver tea sets and one for that French china we purchased last year."

"Very well Sir, we have a telephone engineer in at the moment, there seems to be something wrong with the lines in the village, so they are checking ours as well."

"Really Mrs Mannering, tell Johnson to keep an eye on things."

"I will indeed Sir, so we'll expect you next weekend."

"Yes Mrs Mannering, see you next weekend." He put the phone down. So they were on the estate, the slimy bastards. Still Mrs Mannering knew what to do. They did not have a Johnson on the estate; it was a code for putting his own security team on to it. His staff were really good, all ex security forces all trained by him including Mrs Mannering.

He phoned the Savoy Hotel and booked himself in for an indefinite period, two weeks at least. Let them listen to nothing, unless they thought of bugging the hotel, but they knew that would not be an option. He packed a case and called a taxi, with any luck he should get there before the evening rush and get a good meal in the restaurant before it became filled to capacity.

He had often thought of living there while he was in town, he could afford it, but somehow he needed that bit of privacy that the apartment afforded.

Bland and Boyd had gone to their favourite eating-house as Jean was away, and Amanda was still at her mother's. Bland had Hoi Sin chicken served with new potatoes and salad and Boyd had a hugh burger with chips and salad.

"How's the arm Sir," asked Boyd cramming his mouth full of salad.

"At the moment Boyd it's quite painful, but it should be better soon once the antibiotics begin to work. Trouble is, I'm having a job to cut this chicken, the pain is going right up my arm."

Boyd leaned over and cut the chicken into bite sized pieces.

"There you are Sir," he said.

Much obliged Boyd." Said Bland and continued with his meal. They had a couple of drinks and then Boyd drove Bland home.

"Good night Sergeant," said Bland, "I'll read the reports tonight and let you know the results tomorrow."

"Good night Sir," said Boyd and drove off.

Bland made himself a hot drink and went to bed. He opened the briefcase and started to read the reports. At two in the morning he had finished. No wonder Andrew had told he to put it away and forget it.

Ivan the Terrible turned out to be Percy Lucien la Roche, a member of the aristocracy, just as Bland had suspected. He was a torturer *extraordinaire* and revelled in his art. He had an army of people at his command, people in high places and people in the lowest of low places. His net of intrigue encompassed government ministers, judges, police inspectors, doctors, lawyers, clergymen, gangsters. He had infiltrated all sections of society. He was a very powerful man, no one was beyond his reach, and those who thought they were, or tried to denounce him came to a sticky end. The black book was the key it brought people and places and times together. He would have to see the Super tomorrow. Reading the reports made him feel physically sick. He had tortured young and old alike, even small children, which was the hardest to take. He did not sleep well the rest of the night and his vivid nightmares were full of death and misery.

Chapter Thirty-Seven
Bland Reports

The next morning Bland was very quiet on the way to work. Boyd wondered if he had upset the inspector in some way.

"Is everything alright Sir?" he asked.

"No Boyd, everything is not alright."

"Is it your wound Sir?"

" No Boyd, it's the reports. They are too awful to contemplate."

"Do you want me to read them Sir?"

"No Boyd, no one should have to read them, least of all you."

"The black book wasn't all that bad Sir, was it?"

"It's not the book itself Boyd. You have to understand everything that happens, every dead body that is found, is written up in detail even if the case is never resolved. All the nasty grizzly bits, like eyes being gouged out, hands cut off, rape and murder, slow strangulation, and everything is recorded and confined to the archives. It's not something that the public ever get to know about, not even policemen unless they were involved. The book is the key that ties people to events. It's very dangerous. Andrew is really good, he has tied it all together are revealed the truth. That is why someone is on his case, I hope he's alright."

"What are you going to do Sir?"

"Me, I' m going to see the Super straight away. He's the one who says what is to be done. He gave me the book."

When they arrived at work Bland went straight to see the Super. He sat and waited while the Super read some of Andrew's reports. There were also photographs of the victims, which were particularly harrowing.

"I can't believe this Robert, this little girl had her eyes gouged out and other terrible things done to her."

"And still she didn't die for another four hours," said Bland.

"I feel physically sick Robert."

"I think they are on to Andrew Sir."

"Really Robert – Already!"

"Yes Sir," said Bland, and he told him about the Russians.

"You had better be careful Robert."

"So had you Sir."

"Me? – Of course I'm the one with the book. Has Boyd read any of this?"

"No Sir I thought it best not to let him see it."

"I see, you can't protect him from life Robert."

"I know Sir but this is too awful."

"We'll see," said the Super, "leave everything with me Robert and I'll let you know what I have decided later. It's a pity that we cant get a list of all those who are associated with him, he bound to have one for blackmail purposes."

"Perhaps its another book Sir – it makes you wonder whom you can trust."

"It does Robert, it does. Let's hope that its not another book we're after, God forbid."

"He usually does Sir."

"Look Robert, why don't you and Boyd have a few days leave? I understand you arm is playing up again; the police doctor mentioned it, because the hospital had been in touch with him. Take the rest of the week off and come and see me on Monday and I'll let you know what I am going to do."

"Very well Sir." Bland got up to leave, and as he was going out of the door the Super said,

I'll probable see you on Saturday, my wife is anxious to go, evidently someone has told her that there are some beautiful frocks there."

"Indeed there are Sir, should be a really good turnout." He silently thought that the Super's wife would not be able to get into Jean's dresses, from what he had seen of her at the various functions they had attended she had a sizable arse on her.

"It will be a bit of light relief Robert, in view of what might be ahead of us in the future. I think we will be in need of it."

"Yes Sir," said Bland, and he closed the door and went back to his office.

Chapter Thirty-Eight
Andrew's Gang

As Bland left the office, a door behind the Super opened and Andrew Middleton came in.

"Well Andrew, there's your two men, free for the next few days. Take care of Robert; he's a good man. Do you think he will be willing to help?"

"Oh yes Sir," said Andrew, "I know my man,"

" I'm going to have a word with Boyd, if he is to be in on this caper of yours, he needs to know what is going on. He picked up the phone.

"Boyd, would you please take the Inspector home. That arm has got a nasty infection, then return to the station and come and see me."

Boyd put the phone down and said,

"The old man wants me to take you home and then he wants to see me."

"Perhaps he's going to find you something else to do," said Bland, "although he did say that we were both on leave."

When Boyd dropped him off, Bland went up and lay on the bed. He had not slept well the previous night, and what with the nightmares after reading Andrew's reports, he was feeling really tired. He leaned back and was soon asleep dreaming of funerals, large smelly tomatoes chasing him up the street,

Abigail screaming and jumping on him, and then there was Jean screaming and jumping on Abigail. Then someone was tugging his arm and he heard Boyd's voice softly calling him.

"Wake up Sir, wakeup," he opened his eyes and saw Boyd looking down at him.

"Thank God," he said, "I was just having an awful dream."

"I thought so Sir, you were talking in your sleep, you were telling someone to get off you and leave you alone. We've just made lunch Sir, when you're ready." Boyd then slipped out of the room and went back downstairs before Bland could ask any questions.

Bland got up and went to the bathroom to freshen up. We've he thought, what we've? Has Boyd got some one with him? How did he get in? He doesn't have a key. Perhaps Jean had returned although she said this morning, on the phone that she would be back on Friday.

He went downstairs and could smell cooking and movement in the kitchen. He went in and found that lunch was indeed ready, the table was set for five, there was a huge bowl of fresh salad, new potatoes in mint and butter, sparkling water and red wine. Andrew Middleton was grilling T-bone steaks.

"I don't need to ask how you got in Boyd now that I see that Andrew is here. What's this all about?" Boyd shrugged his shoulders. The doorbell chimed.

"Ah the last two, just in time," said Andrew. Boyd answered the door and came back with a boiler man and a carpet salesman, complete with carpet swatches.

"What has Jean been up to," said Bland.

"Don't worry Robert, these are my men, George and Alan." They both nodded and sat down at the table.

"Explanations after lunch," said Andrew, dishing up the steaks with a knob of garlic butter on the top.

"No wine for you Robert," said Andrew, "you're on antibiotics I hear." Bland frowned at Boyd.

"Not me," said Boyd

"No," said Andrew, "it wasn't Boyd it was the Superintendent." After lunch Andrew and Boyd cleared away and stacked the dishwasher. George and Alan disappeared. They hadn't said a word through lunch.

"What's going on?" demanded Bland.

"Robert why don't you show Boyd and I around your lovely garden?" said Andrew and he held the kitchen door open. Bland said nothing but thought all the more. Boyd had seen the garden hundreds of times. He had eaten many meals in it, why would he want to see it again?

They walked to the brook at the bottom and sat on the bench there.

"Now," said Bland, "What is going on?"

"Well," said Andrew, "My men are searching your house for cameras and listening devices. That's why I didn't say anything inside."

"Oh come off it Andrew," said Bland, "you've been with the secret squirrels too long."

"No Robert my flat is bugged and they've moved onto my estate, pretending to be repairing the telephone lines. My men are keeping an eye on them. You and the Superintendent are next."

"What about Jean?" said Bland.

"I think not," said Andrew, "she's not here and there is no reason to suppose that she is involved in any way.

"She and the boys are coming back on Friday."

"Then we are going to have to move fast," said Andrew.

"There you go with that 'we' again," said Bland.

"You're involved Robert whether you like it or not, still five of us should be enough, six if you count the Superintendent, and I have my men."

"Enough for what?" asked an exasperated Bland

"To get into la Roche's fortress of a country house."

"Are you mad?" said Bland, "I went there once to some do or other it was a Charity Ball for the police fund. La Roche is known for his good works. The Super and I went and it was like getting into Alcatraz. The Super said 'once in, you never get out unless they let you out.' They have got high, electrified fences, alarms on everything, steel shutters on all the windows, and some of the doors. We were frightened to take a pee in case it set an alarm off."

" All good inside information Robert," said Andrew. Suddenly George and Alan appeared. Both Bland and Boyd jumped as they hadn't heard them coming.

"The house is clear Sir," said George.

"Good," said Andrew, "Robert have you a place that we could hide the black book and the reports that nobody would think of looking?"

"Yes," said Bland, "but we don't have the book or the reports. They are back at the station."

"No they're not, " said Andrew, "I brought them with me."

"Very well," said Bland, "follow me." They followed him upstairs into the attic. All the doors in Bland's house were arched and made of oak. They were large and covered in carvings, they were also very thick with huge iron keyholes with large iron keys to match. The door to the attic was no different. The room was empty except for a large carved marble fireplace; an old trunk and two beat up old suitcases.

"In here?" queried Andrew.

"Yes," said Boyd

"Don't worry my boys will soon find it."

"If it pleases you to think so, " said Bland under his breathe. He and Boyd stood back and let them get on with it.

"You alright Boyd," said Bland quietly, "you've not said much, unusual for you."

"The Super made me read the reports, that's why I had to go back. Those photos were just the pits.

"Oh no," said Bland.

"It's all a bit much, isn't it Sir?" Boyd was used to normal crimes, drugs, fraud, the odd robbery, murder but he'd never had contact with the dark side of the world, the underbelly of violence for it's own sake, the real evil that permeated through rich and poor alike. It came as a shock to him.

"It makes the Messenger of Death look like Saint Peter Sir."

"Indeed it does Boyd but it's still a crime."

"I know Sir."

Meanwhile Andrew's men could not find the hiding place.

"Is it behind the panelling or the walls?" said a frustrated Andrew.

"No."

"Up the chimney?"

"No."

"Under the floor boards?"

"No."

"Then where?"

"Give up?" said Bland.

"Oh very well," said Andrew.

"What about you two?" said Bland. George and Allen gave a curt nod.

Bland opened a slim leather wallet he had been holding, and took out a long thin screwdriver with a fine point on the end. In the arch of the door were carvings of leaves and blossoms. Bland unscrewed the centre of three of the blossoms and lifted the whole carving down. This revealed a small keyhole in the point of the arch. He took an elaborate iron key out of the wallet and pushed it into the keyhole. He jiggled it around and there was a sharp click and the panel started to slide down, the protruding key stopped it from disappearing inside the door. Inside were two narrow shelves. Bland took the black book from Andrew and balanced it on one shelve and the reports he split into two and placed them next to each other on the other shelf. When it was arranged to his satisfaction he slid the panel up and locked it. Then he replaced the carvings.

"There you are Andrew, nobody will find them there."

"I'll take charge of those keys," said George stepping forward purposefully.

"Certainly not," said Bland, "my house, my door, my keys. You may have the contents back whenever you please, it's not something that I want in my house." He tucked the wallet in his inside pocket.

"I don't think you understand ," said George moving closer, "we have to have those keys so it's best that you hand them over right away."

"Or else?" said Bland, becoming angry now.

"George," said Andrew coldly, "this is Robert's house and they are his keys. We have access to the papers when ever we need them."

"But - ,"

"No buts George," said Andrew, "lets all go down stairs and have some coffee and plan a little strategy. They gathered around the kitchen table, Boyd made the coffee and Andrew said that they had to find the list of all the people in his organisation. The Super has suggested that you Robert go with him to the ball that La Roche is holding, for the police, fire and ambulance services."

"When?"

"Thursday."

"Thursday! That's tomorrow night."

"Indeed," said Andrew, we've done a bit of reconnaissance and think we know where the safe is."

"He wouldn't put it in a safe Andrew, he'd hide it in plain sight, where he could see it and gloat over the fact that others couldn't."

"I think you are right," said Andrew, he's the sort who would watch a man die of thirst trying to reach a cup of water that was just out of his reach. It would amuse him."

"I don't want to go to the ball," said Bland

"You will if you want to keep Jean safe."

"You're an arsehole Andrew," said Bland.

"I know," said Andrew, "it's one of my better features. There's something that I haven't told you." Both Bland and Boyd hearts sunk.

"We suspect that he has prisoners in that place, members of people's families who he couldn't corrupt any other way. He needs to keep people in line and make them do his bidding without question. The bigger an empire gets the harder it is to maintain. We assume that they are in his fortress, for that is what it is. No visible way in; or out; except the front door."

"That's what I'm worried about," said Bland.

"If you go to the ball with the Super the front door will be open. I promise to have men in the grounds, after all the gates will be open to allow his guests in. Shouldn't be too difficult. We can't afford to make him suspicious or he could kill his hostages."

"Has anybody reported them missing?" asked Boyd.

"Use your loaf dear chap," said Andrew, "why would they, they are not actually missing in the true sense, anyway bringing in the police could easily be their death sentence. As you said before, who can you trust even in the police?"

"Blimey," said Boyd.

Alright," said Bland, "I'll do it."

"Good man," said Andrew, "you'll be going in the Commissioner's car, pick up for you is at seven-forty and the Super is at seven-thirty."

"You were so sure that I would say yes," said Bland.

"Of course," said Andrew, "I know you we have been friends for years." Bland sighed,

"How come," he said, "that you get into more trouble with your friends than you do with your enemies?"

"Just lucky I guess," said Andrew.

"Now," he said, "producing a large plan and spreading it on the table, this is a plan of the estate. The house is enormous and it has lots of cellars, some go beyond the building into this large field area. There are skylights here, and they are made of toughened glass, and are slightly domed. During the war the military took over this estate, and they commissioned these cellars. You can't get in through the skylights because they are in sealed units made of steel. We have to find another way in."

"If, as you say, he has hostages then that is where they will be," said Bland

"That's dreadful," said Boyd.

"Boyd doesn't need to be in on this, does he?" asked Bland.

"Fraid so," said Andrew. "you and the Super on the inside, and Boyd with us on the outside trying to rescue anyone who might be in there."

"Can't you just walk through the front door like anyone else?" said Bland.

"No can do Robert, he knows me and there are just too many cameras and booby traps. Don't worry Robert all you have to do is retrieve the list, we are doing the dangerous bit, breaking in and rescuing."

"Jesus Christ Andrew it's like the middle ages"

"I know Robert but we have to destroy this network before it destroys us. Because you can't be sure whom you can trust I'm bringing my own men. I hope the Super is all right."

"Not him Andrew, I won't have it, I'd trust him with my life."

"That's exactly what you are about to do Robert."

"What am I going to do?" said Boyd.

"You stay will me," said Andrew, "we have to get in and out before he knows that we are there." George and Alan had been very quiet, they had not uttered a word except when George demanded the keys. George suddenly said,

"Should we be involving rank amateurs Sir?"

" Gifted rank amateurs," said Andrew.

"They have no experience Sir," said Alan.

"We can't afford lame ducks Sir," said George.

"Now you both listen here," said Andrew, "If I was in a tight corner the one person I would like at my back is Robert Bland."

"Here, here," shouted Boyd.

"And do you know why?"

"No Sir," said Alan and George.

"Because unlike the security services Robert believes that no one is expendable." Andrew rolled up the plan and turned to Bland

"Well Robert, must be off now, we'll take Boyd with us. All you have to do is enjoy the party and get that evidence."

George and Alan picked up their bags and carpet samples and went out to the van and Andrew followed them. Boyd put on his coat.

"Good luck Sir, don't take any unnecessary risks, especially with your bad arm."

"Oh I'll be all right Boyd, it's you I worry about. You stick to Andrew like glue, he has a knack of coming out of things unscathed, if he fell down the toilet he would come up smelling of roses. You keep out of the firing line, we are after all just coppers, not the SAS."

"Yes Sir, I guess the next time we see each other will be when this job is done. Let's hope it all goes well Cheerio," Boyd ran down the drive and jumped into the van, and it shot off down the drive and into the traffic. Bland shut the door and decided that a stiff drink was in order. He went into the dining room and poured himself a large whiskey.

Chapter Thirty-Nine
Two Visitors

"I'll have a large tonic water, if you don't mind," said a voice behind him. Bland spun around and sitting in an armchair was Giles Jones.

"Christ Giles, you nearly made me drop my drink."

"Sorry Robert, I didn't want to be seen so I slipped in through the back door, while you were seeing them off at the front door. Incidentally I was serious about the drink." Bland poured the tonic water into a tall crystal glass, dropped in a few ice cubes and a slice of lime and handed it to Giles.

"What's a news paper hound doing in my dining room?"

"I know what is happening tomorrow and I want to be part of it."

"Are you completely mad?"

"No, I've also been invited tomorrow night, to take the official photos and some for the paper of course. I need to keep close to you; I'd be no use out in the grounds. Added to which Andrew Middleton wouldn't let me within a mile of any goings on."

"I completely agree with him. I would not be going if I didn't have to."

"You don't have to do anything Robert, just don't notice my presence when I'm hanging around."

"Do you realise what you are getting into?"

"Yes, year's ago when I was a young reporter, Percy fucking La Roche beat up a prostitute and tortured her, it gave him pleasure. I have photos of her after he'd finished with her. She was only a young kid and a friend of mind. She committed suicide when she came out of hospital," he threw an envelope on the table, "take a look at those," he said. Bland wasn't into looking at any more photographs but he picked up the envelope and emptied the contents onto the table. The photos were horrendous.

"Jesus Christ," he said, "look at her face or what's left of it, you can't see her eyes." Her whole body was covered in wounds and cigarette burns. It was obvious that some of her fingers were broken.

"What kind of monster is this man, I've seen some terrible pictures of his victims, and now these, how many more are there that we don't know about? Why didn't she report him?"

"Oh she did, a certain Inspector Colin Jeeves was in charge of the case, and he persuaded her to drop the charges. She wouldn't say why. I'd like to see him go down as well. You see Robert I believe you should always keep faith with your friends, even when they are dead. La Roche has to be stopped, over the years he has spread a pool of fear and misery, other peoples distress and pain is what he lives for."

"All right Giles, I will do my best to ignore your presence. How did you find out about Andrew's plan for tonight?"

"I overheard him talking to his two men in the café before he came here. Don't worry no one else was there, added to which he spoke very quietly, but I can lip read. I learned it from another patient when I was in the clinic drying out."

"If I help you, you must do something for me."

"Anything,"

"We are going to a wedding the Sunday after next. They are an old couple, perhaps you could take a few pictures for them."

"It will be a pleasure – something nice to do for a change. I'm quite good with weddings and children."

"I know that's why I asked."

"Well Robert must go, I've got things to do, I'll see you tomorrow."

"Very well Giles, we have to win this time, I'll shoot him myself if nothing else works."

"Don't worry Robert I'm sure this time it's our turn, I'll avenge Jessica and will be at peace with the world." He collected up his photographs and put them in his pocket.

"Her death has been with me all of these years and I could never do anything about it, but now I can't wait."

Bland showed Giles out and went back to the dining room to finish his drink. He wondered what Jean would say to all this. He was glad that she was away. If they failed tomorrow, what would happen to him and Boyd and Jean? It didn't bear thinking about. He poured himself another drink. He had meant what he had said about Percy fucking La Roche, if all else failed he would kill him himself.

He called Jean and felt reassured that all was well with her and the boys. He went out to dinner and when he got back he laid out his evening clothes for the next night and went to bed. He was soon asleep. He never heard someone enter the room and sit quietly by the bed. He was not aware that someone watched over him all night.

Chapter Forty
D Day Morning

When Bland awoke the chair was empty, he had no idea that he had had a late night visitor.

He showered and dressed and went downstairs to make some breakfast. He picked up the papers as he went through the hall. He made toast and coffee and sat down to enjoy reading the papers. He spread a liberal amount of marmalade on his hot buttered toast and unrolled the papers.

On the front page there was the story of a prisoner who had hung himself in his cell. There was no suicide note and as he had been depressed they assumed it was because his wife had left him. Bland knew that Johnny Briggs hadn't killed himself, he was the original owner of the black book, and he had been killed. The tentacles of Percy Lucian La Roche had reached into the jail and snuffed out the life of someone who might possible testify against him in the future. And so it starts, thought Bland.

Jean phoned and he told her that he was going to the Ball that night as a guest of the Super.

"Well," she said, "have a good time and don't drink too much." Fat chance of that thought Boyd.

"When are you coming back," he asked.

"Why? Are you lonely?" she asked.

"Yes very,"

"Oh Robert," she said softly, "I miss you too. We'll all be back tomorrow night ready for the galleries opening on Saturday."

"Okay Darling, see you then," said Robert.

"Bye, bye Darling," she said, "Love you," And the line went dead.

Bland went back to his papers; he poured himself a second cup of coffee and then something occurred to him. He called Andrew on his mobile

Andrew," he said, "Robert here, just doing the crossword. Seem to have got stuck on a couple. Need to pick your brain. The first one is a military installation, what's that? you can't think of anything. Fat help you are. Try this one. Four letters, clue is air conditioning outlet. Pardon, Oh duct, of course it is. Now try this one, I need this one, as it will set all the others off. The clue is, when all goes dark, it's six three. What do you mean it's easy, oh power cut, I should have thought of that. That was nine down and I can come across from that. Thanks Andrew. Speak to you later." He clicked his mobile off and laid it on the table. Hope Andrew understood that, he thought and went back to his papers.

Meanwhile at the police station the Super was going through some reports when he had a call from the desk sergeant to say that Chief Superintendent Colin Jeeves of the Met was in reception asking to see him.

"Get someone to bring him up," he said and put the phone down. What the hell did he want thought the Super. He disliked Colin Jeeves intensely. Always thought he was as bent as a clockwork orange.

There was a gentle tap on the door and Constable Wilkins announced him and then left.

"Well, well," said the Super, "What brings you here."

"Oh nothing in particular, I was just passing and thought I'd pop in on an old colleague." You never pass this part of town thought the Super, so what do you really want.

"Well sit down, would you care for a glass of something?"

"Don't mind if I do, I'll have whiskey if you've got any."

"Of course," said the Super and he poured two large measures and handed one to his visitor.

"Are you going to La Roche's Ball tonight?" said Jeeves.

"Oh indeed," said the Super

"Who are you taking as your guest?"

"Robert – DCI Bland. He been a bit unwell of late I thought it might cheer him up."

"Robert Bland – don't think I know that name." Liar thought the Super.

"He's a good man," said the Super, "took a bullet in the arm earlier this year."

"I remember it now," said Jeeves. Thought you might, thought the Super

"It was to do with that black book if I've got my facts right. What ever happened to it?"

"Oh Robert didn't want it and passed it on to me, and I passed it on to the MI5 boys. It was more in their keeping. Lord only knows where it is now. Are you going tonight?"

"Oh yes, he's a personal friend of mine la Roche, Does such a lot for the community.

"You don't say?" said the Super. "I only met him once."

"Must go," said Jeeves, got people to see, thanks for the drink, probably see you tonight, don't worry I'll see myself out." And in a flash he was gone.

"So you were looking for the black book you insidious creeping little toady, well you're not going to get it," thought the Super. The death of Johnny Briggs was no surprise this morning. There was nowhere that La Roche couldn't reach. When Jeeves reported back that neither he nor Bland had the black book, maybe that would keep them safe for a while. Tonight would be the watershed, he was glad he had Robert Bland by his side.

After breakfast Bland decided to go to the hospital to visit Steve. His arm was a little better and it wasn't too painful to drive. He stopped on the way and bought a large box of really fancy chocolates from a small shop run by a Belgium chocolatier.

Bland arrived at the ward exactly the same time as Queenie and Teddy.

The nurse pursed her lips and said,

"Only two persons may visit the patient at any one time. Three is not allowed."

"I'll wait in the corridor," said Bland, "and we can swap over later," he turned to the nurse and said, "I suppose that's alright?"

"Only two," she said, "It doesn't matter which two," and walked off in a huff.

Bland popped the chocolates on the bed and went and sat in the corridor. While he was waiting he watched people going about their business totally unaware of him sitting there.

Two men turned into the corridor and looked up and down and then signalled to someone to come forward. Bland looked up interested, and around the corner came Percy bloody La Roche. He turned down the corridor so didn't notice Bland sitting there. All three of them disappeared into a private room.

Well, well, thought Bland, who are you visiting so secretively?

Teddy appeared and said,

"Your turn Mr Bland, them chocolates are something else, all in their little gold cups and coloured silver paper, they is something to behold."

"Good," said Bland, "Teddy thee men went into that room down there, number four B. Let me know when they come out again."

"Do you know 'em Mr Bland?"

"Well I know Percy Lucien La Roche, I'm going to his do tonight with the Superintendent. It's a big charity bash, not something I'm looking forward to."

"You watch your step Mr Bland, 'e's about as evil as anyone can get. Don't you get mixed up wiv 'im."

"I don't intend to," said Bland, "now let's go and see Steve."

When he got to the bedside he noticed that the top layer of chocolates had been eaten, and there were empty foil cups and silver paper and little pleated brown cups all over the bed.

"Have a chocolate," said Queenie.

"Don't mind if I do," said Bland choosing a coffee cream, "thank-you."

"Thanks ever so for the chocolates," said Steve, "I can't remember the last time I had such posh chocolates."

"You're welcome," said Bland, "how are you feeling now?"

"Oh much better, thank-you Sir, the operation was a success and I have more movement in my arm now." Bland stayed for another ten minutes chatting and then he got up to leave.

"Better let Teddy back in," he said, "I expect he's getting restless now."

"Thanks for coming," said Steve, "and thanks for the sweets."

"My pleasure," said Bland, "I'll see you all on Saturday." He went outside and Teddy said, "They all came out five minutes ago Mr Bland, and they was in a right 'urry."

"Thanks Teddy, you'd better go back in now before Queenie polishes off all the chocolates."

"That's 'er all over, she can't stop 'erself, no wonder she's got such a big arse. I'll see you Saturday Mr Bland, and don't you get mixed up with you know who," and he went through the swing doors into the ward."

Bland moved carefully down the corridor, looking around to make sure that no one saw him. He slipped into Room four B.

"Mr Bland," said a weak voice from the bed, "what are you doing 'ere?"

"Why it's Dave from the Chippy," exclaimed Bland in surprise. The Chippy was one of the best fish and chip shops in town. Everybody went there, including Teddy and Arthur.

"How come you're in hospital?" said Bland, but as he got closer to the bed he could see that Dave had received a severe beating, and it looked as though he had just received another one. There was blood everywhere.

"Who did this," said Bland

"Don't know Sir, they just burst in." Bland rang the bell for the nurse, and when she came he explained that he had seen three men come in when he was waiting to visit another patient further up the corridor, but he had not seen them come out again. The nurse called the hospital security and Bland got up to go.

"You can't go Sir," she said, "You'll have to speak to the police."

"I am the police," he said and handed her his card, "I'll be back later." Before he left he leaned over Dave and said very quietly,

"I know who it was, was this beating a reminder to keep quiet?"

"They've got my little girl," sobbed Dave.

"Jesus," said Bland, "this bastard has got to be stopped once and for all," and he left the room in a rage.

He went down to his local watering hole and found Boyd waiting for him.

"Thought you'd be here Sir," said Boyd.

"I'm a creature of habit," said Bland, "have you ordered?"

"No, Sir I thought I'd wait for you."

"Right," said Bland, "my treat, you order and I'll have steak and kidney pie and a pint of bitter and what ever you are having, he took some notes out of his wallet and passed them to Boyd, "that should take care of it."

"That's too much," said Boyd.

"I've allowed for the fact that we might have a sweet. There won't be much tonight, bits of things on sticks, not that I'll feel like eating and you

Boyd will be outside and won't be getting anything, so you had better make the most of it now."

They settled in their favourite corner and Bland told Boyd what had happened at the hospital.

"So he has got people hostage."

"Looks like it Boyd."

"Poor sods."

"Poor sods indeed Boyd, lets hope that they are still alive."

"Oh don't say that Sir," said Boyd. They sat in silence until their meal arrived, lost in their own thoughts.

"Does Mrs Bland know about tonight Sir?"

"Well she knows that I am going to the ball with the Super, but that's all. She told me not to drink too much."

"I reckon she's going to have a thing or two to say when she gets back, especially as you did not tell her about your wound opening up again."

"I'll face that when the time comes Boyd."

After lunch Boyd went off to meet Andrew and Bland went back to the hospital. He had to make a statement, and he wanted to see Dave again.

When all the formalities were done, he went and sat with Dave.

The nurse fussed about for a while and then she left the room. Outside was a seven-foot policeman guarding the door. A bit late in the day thought Bland.

"How long has she been gone Dave?"

"Two weeks Sir, if you make it official they will kill her. Please for God's sake say nothing."

"Don't worry Dave, nobody is going to make it official."

"Sir I know something that he doesn't know I know. I'll tell you but I'll deny that I told you if I'm ever questioned."

"That's understood," said Bland.

"There is a list."

"I know."

"I know where it is."

"Where."

"It's behind a picture of his ex wife on his desk. He hated her so why would he keep her picture on his desk. I went up to his house with a big order for a party. He was having a fish and chip night. It was for forty people. I left the order in the kitchen and went up to his room to get paid, as I got to the door I saw him folding sheets of paper and putting them in the back of the photograph. He didn't see me at the door, when he moved away from the desk I knocked on the open door and went in."

"If he didn't see you why is he beating you up and why has he taken your child?"

"Ah well Sir, there was someone else in the room that night, Gloria Olsen, you know the girl that was found raped and murdered the next morning under the arches. He knew I had seen her and he took my baby to keep me quiet."

"I see," said Bland, "don't worry Dave this will go no further. If I can retrieve that list maybe things will turn to our advantage. If he has people they have to be our first priority and nothing must endanger their safety. Try not to worry and I'll come and see you in a couple of days." He got up and left.

Once he was home he put the alarm clock on in case he failed to wake in time. He lay on the bed and drifted off, later he would wake up and get a shower and dress, and wait for the car to collect him. Outside a car was parked in the road under a tree and someone was watching the house.

Chapter Forty-One
The Ball

The Super got into the back seat of the limousine and directed the driver to collect DCI Bland. He leaned back and sighed. His wife was very put out that he was not taking her to the ball. Why was he taking another policeman? She wanted to know. He tried to tell her that it was more of a business occasion than an actual ball, but she would have none of it. He was glad to leave the house and get away from the nagging.

They picked up Bland and the car sped away. Apart from wishing each other 'Good Evening' they sat in silence, finally the Super said,

"Not looking forward to this tonight Robert, how are we expected to find this list?"

"I know where it is Sir."

WHAT?"

"I know where it is, but I can't tell you who told me because Percy fucking La Roche has his child."

"Good grief Robert, he has got hostages, when did you find out?"

"A couple of hours ago Sir."

"Where is it?"

"It's in his study so we need to get in there."

"Leave it to me Robert, I'll get him to invite us in."

"Are you sure Sir?"

"I'll make sure of it Robert, I have to, I'll tell you what Robert I feel a little better, at least now I've got a purpose."

"Yes Sir," said Bland but he thought it was not going to be that easy; La Roche was nobody's fool.

The limousine swept up La Roche's drive and stopped level with the steps. They got out and ascended the red-carpeted steps and their invitations were checked and they joined the milling crowd.

"Let's go to the buffet Robert, I feel like a drink and I haven't eaten all day. I didn't feel like it." They pushed their way through the crowd. The buffet seemed to go on forever, Percy La Roche did not stint, especially on these large public functions.

"What would Sir like?" said a waiter who looked as though he had an unpleasant smell under his nose. He held a large gold rimmed white plate in a table napkin in one hand, and a silver fork poised in the other.

"Ah," said the Super, "I'm really hungry," and he had his plate filled.

"Robert, how are you supposed to eat your food and hold your drink at the same time?"

"There are tables in the next room Sir," said the waiter.

"Good," said the Super, "Get your food Robert and lets go while we can still get a seat." They made their way into the next room and settled on a table in the corner.

"Damn good food," said the Super.

"Very nice," said Bland who only had a couple of sausage rolls, which he nibbled at. He had eaten well at lunchtime and wasn't hungry, anyway he had an awful empty feeling in his stomach, a feeling of impending doom.

"Where's La Roche Sir?"

"He hasn't made an appearance yet Robert, he likes to make a grand entrance."

"Do you know where his study is?"

"No Robert – don't worry, he'll take us there we won't have to look for it."

"I wish I had your confidence Sir."

"You worry too much Robert."

. . . .

Outside in the grounds Andrew and Boyd and Andrew's men were moving silently through the tree towards the house. They had just reached the skylights in the grass. Andrew's men tried to see what was below with their flashlights and infra red cameras but they couldn't see anything. Over the years the domes and become pitted and the glass was ingrained with dirt.

"Put those lights out," hissed Andrew, "for God's sake do you want everyone to know we are here."

"If anyone is down there Sir there's no way of knowing."

"Very well," said Andrew, "let's find the generator, the lights have to go off at nine o' clock." They moved on, there was a crack team of commandos in the grounds who were just waiting for Andrew's signal. At that moment, the generator would go off and they would blow one of the domes open, other men would go through the back windows on the ground floor and men on the roof would abseil down and enter some of the top windows.

The generator was inside a huge cage but it took them no time at all to get in. Everyone knew what he or she had to do. It was just a question of waiting now,

Boyd lay in the grass with the others and waited. Just to his right a light suddenly went on in one of the domes.

"Look Sir, he said to Andrew, "there's a light in that dome." He and Andrew and one of Andrew's men slithered on their bellies across the grass and peered carefully through the glass to see what was going on below. It was not good. La Roche was there and he was torturing a young man who was strapped to a table. Andrew made Boyd look away. As the red-hot poker went into the man's flesh he let out a scream, but it was a silent scream as the glass was so thick no sound could be heard.

"What's going on?" asked Boyd.

"You don't want to know," said Andrew, "go and help the men at the generator, remember it must go off at exactly nine o' clock for seven minutes."

" Right," said Boyd and he moved off running bent over, so the bushes that were dotted here and there among the trees would hide him..

Suddenly La Roche looked at his watch and realised the time, he threw the poker down and he and his henchman left, turning out the light as they went. Now he goes to greet his guests as though nothing has happened, thought Andrew. He spoke into his headpiece telling his men to make sure that the explosion went off at exactly nine o, clock, and with any luck they would think it was the generator blowing up, and wouldn't look for anything else.

Chapter Forty-Two
Showtime

Giles had arrived to take the photographs and he saw Bland and the Super and came over.

"Well he should make an appearance any time now. I was booked for eight-thirty," he said.

"Good," said the Super, "Robert and I are fed up with hanging around. Where have all these young girls come from, they would appear to be half naked."

"He must be on his way," said Giles, "the girls are for his guests."

"Well I never did," said the Super, "turning a charity ball into a knocking shop."

"That's La Roche for you," said Giles.

"Here he comes now," said Bland, "coming down the steps with his entourage. You're on Giles." Giles laughed and went across and started taking photographs. La Roche started to greet his guests, moving from one group to the next

"Come on Robert, its show time," said the Super, "Let's get in line and say the right words."

La Roche's eyes flitted around, although he was greeting and talking to his guests. He watched all that was going on. He was like an evil snake waiting to pounce on his prey.

Suddenly he caught sight of Bland and the Super coming towards him. He excused himself from the local mayor and made his way towards them.

"Welcome, welcome," he said, "so glad you could come. This must be DCI Bland, welcome to you. Gosh this is such a crush, it's so nice of people to turn out, but you can't hear yourself think. Come up to my study and have a quiet drink." They followed him through the crowd and up the curved stairway. Bland made the Super give him his invitation card.

"What do you want it for?"

"I'm going to fold our two cards together and when I remove the list I'm going to replace it with the invitation cards." They reached the top of the stairs and turned into a quiet hallway.

"Come on in," said La Roche swinging the double doors open, "let's be comfortable. Shut the door there's a good chap," he said to Bland. Bland closed the door and as he did so he noticed Giles hovering further down the hall.

"What's you poison?" asked la Roche

"Brandy," said the Super

"Scotch," said Bland. La Roche poured the drinks and handed them out and then sat down in his huge leather chair behind a large antique desk. Bland and the Super sat on chairs on the other side of the desk feeling as though they were up before the headmaster. Bland noticed the photograph on the desk. He did not look at his watch in case La Roche picked up on it. He hoped Andrew had picked up his message and understood it, and that the lights would go out at nine o' clock.

"We are not keeping you from your guests are we?" said the Super.

"Not at all, not at all my dear chap," said La Roche, "I've got lots of people looking after their needs they don't need me. The drink is flowing and the dancing has just begun, people won't notice that I am not there." He refilled their glasses and said,

"Now tell me about the black book."

"Nothing to tell really," said the Super.

"Come on Robert, I may call you that mayn't I?"

"Of course," said Robert stiffly, "the book's not very exciting in it's own right. It's just the ramblings of a small time petty criminal who is no longer with us."

"Come now," said La Roche watching Bland closely, "you were wounded."

"Indeed I was," said Bland, "and I'm still suffering from it. That part of the book was easily understood."

" But if there was a translator, such as Andrew Middleton, that would make a difference, " said La Roche slyly, never taking his eyes off Bland, "someone who could make up reports and profiles and provide evidence."

"Yes, said Bland, "but you'd have to speak to Mr Middleton about that."

"You don't have the book then?"

"Certainly not," said Bland, "I've got enough on my plate with the Messenger of Death case."

Suddenly there was an explosion and the lights went out

"Good grief," said the Super, "your generator has blown up."

"Stay where you are," said La Roche in a cold voice, all pretence at friendliness was gone now, "I'll be back in a minute," and he staggered out of the room. Bland jumped up, and grabbed the photograph and got under the desk. He swiftly opened the back and exchanged the invitations for the lists. He clicked the back into place and scrabbled out from under the desk and placed it back on the desk.

"What on earth are you doing Robert," said the Super

"I slipped over Sir and knocked something down. I've got it now."

La Roche, La Roche," shouted the Super, "confound the man where has he got to. You'd think that they would have some form of emergency lighting in a place like."

"Come on Sir," said Bland, "let's try and find the others." They made their way to the door and into the hallway. They edged their way along the hall, to the top of the stairs. They could see light coming from below. Masses of candles in huge candelabras were being set out in the ballroom and the buffet and in the main hallway and entrance. There was a hub of people talking and laughing, not at all fazed by the sudden plunge into darkness.

As they made their way down the staircase Bland whispered to the Super that he had the lists and it was time to get out – fast.

"You have?" said the Super in disbelief, "well lets go." As they reached the bottom of the stairs the lights went on again and everybody cheered.

Giles had been waiting at the bottom of the stairs and looked relieved to see them.

"Not leaving are we?" said a cold voice behind them; they turned to see La Roche immediately behind them.

"Damn it La Roche, where did you disappear to?" said the Super.

"Just went to make sure that the lights come back on again," smiled La Roche, but the smile was cold, "now he said, I'm afraid that I can't let you leave Superintendent, not so early in the evening, the party has just begun."

Chapter Forty~Three
Face off

Bland was worried that La Roche knew something, what if they had infra-red cameras in his study, would they work if the electricity was off? Bland was not a technical man. At least, he thought he had got under the table to make the swap, surely he couldn't be seen under there.

"I could do with something to eat," said Bland, "what about you Sir, they have an excellent buffet here." He was mindful that the Super had already consumed a large plateful of food, but it was the only thing he could think of to get away from La Roche.

"Good thinking," said the Super.

"Very good thinking," said La Roche. As he edged the Super towards the buffet Bland wondered how they were going to get away; La Roche's henchmen, who were at every door, were watching them. Giles followed them to the buffet.

"What was that explosion?" asked Bland.

"Don't know," said Giles, "it seemed to come from the wooded area. I was standing on the terrace and saw a flash."

"It had to be the generator," said the Super

Behind them La Roche had been surrounded by a bevy of giggling girls who dragged him to the dance floor.

"How are we going to get out?" said Bland, "there are La Roche's men on every door."

"We could just try walking out onto the terrace, people are going in and out all the time," said Giles.

"Hadn't you better go and take some photographs of La Roche with the girls, he could get suspicious if you don't," said Bland, "Look at that prancing ninny, what does he look like swirling his silver topped cane?"

"I would prance about a bit if I was surrounded by that collection of half naked beauties," said the Super wistfully.

"Give me five minutes," said Giles, "and then make for the terrace," and then he went to take photos of La Roche.

"Where's the list?" whispered the Super.

"Lists," said Bland, "they're inside my shirt."

"Good," said the Super.

"Not good," said Bland, "we need to get out of here and get them to a safe place." The next five minutes seemed like an eternity. Giles took masses of photos and in the end La Roche got irritated and told him to go and take pictures of his guests. Giles took pictures of the Lord Mayor and his Lady and lots of minor celebrities gradually making his way back to Bland and the Super. Giles took a picture of them saying,

"Now just wander slowly out onto the terrace, I'll join you in a couple of minutes." Bland and the Super walked slowly out onto the terrace and waited.

"Why are we waiting for that old hack of a newspaper man?" said the Super

"I couldn't say," said Bland, "but there is always safety in numbers." Giles appeared,

"Right let's get going, I take it that you got what you came for?"

"Yes," said Bland as they descended the terrace steps. They made their way across the lawns towards the main entrance.

"Suddenly the sky lit up with another explosion and people could be seen running among the trees in the woodland.

"Andrew's having a field day," said Bland. At that moment the huge main gates swung shut.

"Can't get out that way," said the Super.

"Better make for the wooded area," said Bland, "at least Andrew and his men are there."

Out of the semi-darkness stepped La Roche and two of his men.

"Going so soon," he said.

"Look here La Roche," said the Super determined to bluff it out, "what the hell is going on? You have explosions going off over there, and we are going to see in anyone needs help, and to investigate. That's what policemen do you know."

"What goes on, on my own private land has nothing to do with you, so let's return to the party, after all that is why you're here, is it not?" People were pouring out of the house, and drunken revellers surrounded them: they had come to see what they thought were fireworks going off. Bland took the opportunity to run for it. One of La Roche's men made a lunge at him but got entangled with two of the drunken dancing girls and all three of them crashed to the ground. The other man went to follow Bland but Giles jumped on his back and they hit the ground. La Roche raced after Bland, he was younger and faster and caught up with Bland as he entered the woods, which were on a steep slope. Bland turned and faced La Roche.

"You can't get away from me," snarled La Roche, "there's nowhere you could hide that I couldn't find you, " and he drew a short slim sword from the cane he was carrying. Bland's heart sank, he had no weapon so was at La Roche's mercy.

Now," said La Roche pointing the sword at Bland's chest, "where is the book and the reports?"

"I don't have any black book and I know nothing about reports," said Bland. He felt at a disadvantage because they were on the steepest part of a slope and La Roche was above Bland looking down on him.

"I don't doubt that you don't have the black book but I guarantee that you know where it is."

"Why me?" asked Bland, trying to keep his balance on the slippery slope.

"I know where the brains are, that stupid policeman you're with wouldn't have it. Andrew Middleton would make sure that it wasn't in his possession, so that only leaves you. Don't deny it again as it will be the worst for you. I'm willing to pay handsomely for it; perhaps money is not your thing. Maybe there is something else you'd like. There's nothing that I can't get for you."

Bland suddenly felt old and tired and wanted this to end, if La Roche was going to kill him, so be it.

"I'll tell you what I would like, it's to get my hands around your scrawny little neck and squeeze the life out of you, so go to hell you fucking crazy man."

"Nobody dares to call me crazy," shouted La Roche and lunged at Bland stabbing him in the shoulder, he had aimed at his heart but Bland was sliding down the slope on some very sticky mud.

"No," shouted Bland, "they call you Ivan the Terrible."

"No", shrieked La Roche, and lunged again at Bland. This time he aimed lower and drove the sword into Bland's side just above his waist. Bland lost his footing and started to slide backwards down the slope gathering speed. He put his hands down and tried to grab the odd bush as he passed. Then he crashed into a large tree and fell on his side. La Roche was slipping down the slope waving his sword like a frenzied maniac, and screaming obscenities, he was now totally out of control. He raised his sword above his head to get maximum thrust and to Bland's amazement he saw a figure loom up out of the darkness behind La Roche. Strong arms came up and hands closed over La Roche's and with a short sharp thrust the sword was plunged into La Roche's own stomach. La Roche screamed in agony and the figure kicked him down the slope where La Roche continued to scream. It was unbearable

"Make him stop," shouted Bland

"Very well Sir" said the figure and in the next moment Bland heard a shot ring out and echo through the trees and La Roche was silent.

"Jesus, whispered Bland, "that wasn't what I meant." The figure was bending over him,

"He would have died anyway Sir, it was like putting down a sick animal."

"Well, said Bland, "he was plenty sick."

"Look Sir I'm going to get help. You lay as still as you can as you are losing a lot of blood." He put a large wadding bandage over the wound in Bland's side and told him to hold it there.

"Now Sir lay as still as you can, unfortunately I have only one dressing with me. I'm sorry that I didn't get to you sooner but I got entangled in a kind of scrum further up and lost sight of you." He hurried off and Bland lay there, here it was quiet but he could hear gunshots, people shouting, ambulance's sirens and a couple of explosions in the distance,

He realised that he was too weak to get up so he would just have to remain there until he was rescued. What was that God-awful smell, he realised that he was laying in it. He remembered that La Roche kept deer and he assumed that he was laying in one of their marking places and toilets. After a few minutes he heard something moving and in the gloom and he could see a huge buck coming carefully towards him. Please God, thought Bland, don't let him do his business on me. The great creature bent down, Bland heard his antlers clack on the tree. He could feel its breath on his face. Bland kept his eyes tight closed. The creature sniffed him and then licked his face with a big wet dribbly tongue. It remained there a minute or so and then moved away. Bland lay there with his face covered with reindeer spit, he was glad he was laying on side that was bleeding as the lists were in his shirt on the other side, and he didn't want them covered in blood.

The pain seemed to be fading; he seemed to have pins and needles everywhere. He shivered, he was getting very cold now and he could hear people coming nearer and calling out.

"Sir where are you?" It was Boyd. Bland heard him and was pleased that at least Boyd was all right. He had no strength to answer and succumbed to exhaustion and cold and closed his eyes.

When Boyd found him he was laying cold and still.

"Come on Sir," said Boyd, "don't die on us, what will Mrs Bland say, she'll kill the both of us." Bland however did not hear him Bland was past hearing anything.

Chapter Forty-Four
Mopping up Time

At one o' clock in the morning the telephone rang in Jean's house. David answered it and told the caller that they would come straight away. He went and woke Seth. Jean came out of her room,

"Who on earth was that?" he said.

"It was Boyd Mum, Robert's in hospital I think his wound has opened up again."

"Really," said Jean, "why didn't he call earlier?"

"They were out on a job and I think that complications have set in."

"He went to a ball with the Superintendent," said Jean, "I do hope he hasn't fallen down drunk and hurt himself."

"I said that we would go straight away Mum."

"Oh very well," said Jean, "we're all packed ready to go tomorrow, so we'll get dressed, you boys load up the car and I'll make coffee and sandwiches to take with us."

"Why are we going now?" whispered Seth when they were loading up the car.

"I didn't tell Mum but he's been badly hurt. Boyd's frantic, he is not sure that he will survive. He thought he was dead when he found him in a pool of blood. I think it is touch and go."

"Christ," said Seth, "let's get a move on."

One the way to London the boys sat in the back and had coffee and sandwiches and later David took over the wheel so that Jean could have some much needed coffee.

When they arrived at the hospital he pulled into the car park and collected change from the others.

"I know they charge during the day but I'm not sure about the night time.

"Well really," said Jean, "fancy having to pay."

As they went into reception the place was alive with policemen and the media. Everybody talking at once, Boyd was waiting for them and he guided them through the crowd. They went up in the lift and when the doors opened there were more policemen.

"This is Mrs Bland," said Boyd.

"And who are they? " said a large sergeant pointing at the boys.

"They are his adopted sons," said Boyd. The policemen stepped aside and let them through. They went down the corridor to a waiting room at the end.

"Had to say that said Boyd "otherwise they would not have let you in."

"That's okay," said the boys. As they went in the Super came over to greet them.

"Now you mustn't worry dear lady, he's still unconscious, but he's more stable now."

"Unconscious," said Jean in panic, "how did he get to be unconscious?"

"Did Boyd tell you he was run through with a sword, twice in fact, Percy Lucien La Roche wanted information that Robert was not prepared to give, look on the bright side, we rescued all the hostages unharmed, at least by us.

Any harm they had suffered was at the hands of La Roche. Robert got the lists and La Roche's whole rotten empire is collapsing."

"Hostages, empire," said Jean, she had no idea what he was talking about.

"I must see him," she said.

"Now, now don't upset yourself my dear, he is unconscious he won't know you're there."

"I don't care," said Jean, "I insist on seeing him." The Super could see that Jean was getting very upset and arranged for her to sit by the bedside for a while.

Bland was in an oxygen tent and his breathing seemed very laboured, he seemed to be covered in tubes. Jean sat down and tears streamed down her face. All those wasted years when they could have been together, and when at last they were this had to happen.

Bland looked dead, his face was like stone and he was so still.

"Oh Robert," she whispered, "please don't leave me now I couldn't bear it."

Jean suddenly became aware of a tapping noise someone was using a laptop. She hadn't noticed that there was another bed in the other half of the room. A rather battered man hit the last key and said,

"Gone at last."

"You're that newspaper man called Giles aren't you?"

"Yes, and you are the famous fruit thrower, Mrs Bland, if I'm not mistaken. My story with pictures has just gone to press. I have sold it to a really good paper this time, and they have offered me a permanent place with them."

"Oh well done," said Jean, "Robert thinks very well of you. Tell me what happened."

"How long have you got?"

"Until Robert wakes up." Giles told her about the black book, the reports, Andrew Middleton, the hostages and how they got trapped at the ball. They had found thirty hostages alive but some of them had been badly tortured. There were six children among them but thankfully none of them had been tortured, but two of them looked as though they had been starved. In one torture chamber they had found pieces of bodies and Boyd had been physically sick so Andrew had sent him to find Bland.

"When we were cornered by La Roche and two of his men, Robert made a run for it, but La Roche caught up with him and stabbed him. One of the men got tangled up with a bunch of drunken girls and they all finished up on the floor. I jumped on the back of the other man and got the shit beaten out of me for my trouble. When the other man disentangled himself from the girls the Super jumped on his back and they both went down. The weight of the Super broke the man's arm and the Super remained sitting on him until the police arrived. Poor old Boyd went frantic when he found Robert he thought he was dead. Don't worry Mrs Bland Robert is a tough old bird he'll pull through." They chatted on for another half an hour then Jean settled down to watch Robert and Giles nodded off to sleep.

Chapter Forty-Five
Abigail Merchant

The swing doors opened slowly and there stood Abigail Merchant. She and Jean caught sight of each other at the same moment.

"You!" they both said in unison.

"You get out of here, you bitch," hissed Jean getting up.

"You're the one who threw rotten fruit at me," snarled Abigail

"I'll do worse than that," said Jean moving around the end of the bed.

"Ladies," said Giles waking up, "ladies please."

"Oh yeah," said Abigail, "just you try, you shrivelled up old bag, you tricked Robert into marrying you."

"You trollop," said Jean through her teeth, "Have you no shame, look at yourself, you know what they say, too much make-up and too few clothes is a sign of a desperate woman, and boy are you desperate, creeping around a married man, how sad is that."

"How dare you," shouted Abigail.

"I dare," said Jean and she swung her shoulder bag around three time and brought it down on Abigail's head with a sickening thud. Abigail screamed and staggered unsteadily towards Jean. The Super suddenly appeared behind Abigail, and he put his arm around her waist, and lifted her off the ground left the room with her screaming with rage and using language that he hadn't heard since his youth when he was a young copper on the beat in the east end.

"Take this woman and escort her from the hospital," he said to a large sergeant on the door.

"Right away Sir," said the sergeant and he picked up Abigail in a fireman's lift and disappeared down the corridor with Abigail banging him on the back and shouting abuse.

"I've said it before," said the Super, "and I'll say it again that woman is definitely unhinged. We can't have people like her in the hospital it's upsetting for the patients."

Jean sank down in the chair besides Bland and started to cry again. She couldn't bear the thought that she might lose Robert and that woman really was the last straw. What an utter cow. Suddenly Jean was aware that Bland's eyes were fluttering.

"Oh Robert," she said, "my dear Robert."

"What's all that bloody noise?" said Bland and his eyes closed, his head fell to one side and he fell into a deep sleep. His breathing became regular.

A nurse came in and bustled around, she removed the oxygen tent and told Jean that he would be all right now, as he was no longer unconscious and was sleeping peacefully.

"It's good for him," she said, "it's the start of the healing process. I suggest that you go home now and get some sleep and come back again about noon, he should be awake by then."

"Thank-you Nurse," said Jean, "I'm sorry about the scene, she's a dreadful woman."

"That's all right Mrs Bland, I don't know how she got past security, I know all about her, she's a regular man eater. Now you go home, have a rest, put on a pretty frock and dry your tears. He won't want to see an unhappy swollen face when he wakes up later."

Jean thanked the nurse again, collected the boys and went home.

They made breakfast and sat around the table reading the early morning papers.

"Jesus, said David, "look at the pictures in this one."

"That's Giles," said Jean, "he's in hospital with Robert."

"Who was that woman?" asked Seth.

"Oh she fancies Robert," said Jean and she told them about the fruit throwing at the funeral. They burst into laughter.

"Oh Mum," said David, "I would have loved to have been there."

"Me too," said Seth.

"Well," said Jean, "After breakfast I'm going to get a shower, unpack, and get your rooms ready, it will help pass the time."

"This is a gorgeous house," said Seth.

"I know," said Jean, "I just love it, but I couldn't be here without Robert."

"Jean would you like me to stay a little longer?" said Seth.

"Definitely not," said Jean, "you boys must go and take your chances. I wouldn't hear of your staying, so please don't mention it again."

At twelve o' clock they were back at the hospital. Bland was awake and talking to Boyd. Jean and the boys crowded around the bed.

"Only two visitors per patient," said the nurse. Seth and David went and sat with Giles asking him a million questions. Boyd got up.

"You don't have to go," said Jean.

"I must Mrs Bland the Super is expecting me back. Good-bye Sir, good-bye Mrs Bland, I'm pop in tomorrow."

As Boyd walked down the corridor he felt relieved and glad that Bland was alive. They were a partnership and got on well. They understood each other and that didn't happen with most police partnerships.

"Oh Darling," said Jean, "I was so frightened."

"So was I," said Bland, "I thought I was a goner and then officer Campbell loomed up and killed La Roche. Evidently Andrew assigned him too stay close to me once we had made our plans. I was totally unaware of his presence."

"It's a pity that he didn't get to you sooner," said Jean.

"Wasn't his fault, a party of drunks collided with us, that's when I made a run for it, but he got knocked over and when he got up he couldn't see where we had gone. Then he heard La Roche screaming at me and by the time he got there La Roche had already stabbed me twice. Still all's well that ends well."

"We came as soon as Boyd phoned us, by the way they are your adopted sons it was the only way Boyd could get them in."

"That's all right with me," said Bland, "I think it's good to have two grown up sons, especially if they become famous. Do you think that they will take care of us in our old age?"

"Oh Robert," said Jean laughing.

"You know Jean I had a weird dream,"

"Really," said Jean, "what did you dream?"

"It was really strange, it looked like a handbag fight between two women. The language was dreadful, it sounded like two old fishwives."

"Really," said Jean, "well if I was you I would forget all about silly dreams, especially if you want to live a long and happy life."

"I see," said Bland, "Did you bring me any grapes?"

"No," said Jean, "we just brought ourselves, we mistakenly thought that that would be enough, if it isn't we can soon go home," she said haughtily.

"That's what I like to see," said Bland, "your eyes flashing."

"Oh you," laughed Jean.

"Are the boys all right?"

"I think so," said Jean, "Seth offered to stay and defer his trip because of what has happened, but I told him that I wouldn't hear of it."

"He's a nice chap Jean, David could do worse."

"I know," said Jean, "but David seems to walk about with blinkers on."

"Never mind Jean, things always happen in their own time. Nothing can be rushed.

The nurse came in and threw everybody out so that Bland could get some rest

"He's very ill and quite weak due to the loss of blood and we don't want him to get too tired, he won't get better that way. Sleep is what he needs." Bland suspected that the nurse would be please if all her patients slept all day, to be woken only at meal times. She would be even happier if there were no visitors to upset her rules and regulations. That would be her heaven – complete control.

Chapter Forty-Six
A Visit from Big Harry

Teddy, Arthur, Queenie and Quentin had been in the Galleries since six in the morning, tomorrow was their opening day and everything had to be just so. They had stopped for a well-earned breakfast and were reading the papers.

"Poor Mr Bland," said Queenie.

"Told 'im not to get mixed up wiv La Roche," said Teddy.

"Well someone 'ad to, if everything you read and hear about La Roche is true."

"Are we going to get Steve this morning?" asked Arthur.

"Yus," said Teddy, "we'll go and get him now, we've about finished here.

"You'll be alright now won't you Quentin?"

"Of course," said Quentin, "everything here is tickady-boo. Auntie Queenie and I will be fine." Suddenly they felt a draft blow through from the workshop,

"I'll have to keep that back entrance locked," muttered Teddy, "we've got to stop people just wandering in.

"Allo boys," said the undeniable voice of Big Harry.

"Allo 'Arry, said Teddy, " to what do we owe this 'onour?"

"Thought I'd pop in and let you know what I have arranged for Lenny the Dip."

"What's that?" said Arthur.

"Well little Arfur, I let 'im know that I knew that he had been flapping 'is mouth to the police about things which don't concern 'im. I'd showed 'im how disappointed I was." I bet you did thought Teddy.

"Then little Arfur, I suggested that he might like to go to Scotland to look after my holiday cabin. It needs a good clean. He seemed a little shy at first, so I explained that it was either a first class ticket on a sleeper arriving in Scotland this morning, or travelling in a box in the luggage department. He took the first class ticket, which was very wise of 'im." Quentin held his handkerchief tightly over his mouth to stifle a frightened squeak he made.

"If he tries to come back before I tell 'im I 'ave someone up there who will make 'im see the error of his ways." Quentin's eyes bulged and he kept his handkerchief tightly over his mouth to suppress any sound coming out.

"Well it's nice to know that 'e won't be around tomorrow," said Teddy.

"Indeed," said Big Harry, "we can't 'ave little toe-rags like 'im ruining our special occasion. I've got me speech ready for tomorrow Teddy and my lady wife is well excited. By the way she loves the cocktail cabinet, I earned a few brownie points with that. She 'as parties all the time now and is a very 'appy lady, and if she's 'appy I'm 'appy. You done good there boys, Well I must be off now, places to go and people to see. I'll see you tomorrow about an hour before opening time."

"See you then," said Teddy and he escorted Big Harry out of the building. When he returned he said that he had locked up so that nobody else could get in.

"Uncle Teddy do you think he might actually kill Lenny?"

"Well Quentin, its 'ard to say, a lot depends on 'is mood. In the past he wouldn't have thought twice, but nowadays 'e wants to be thought well of.

He wants to be respectable, he now moves in different circles and wouldn't like to be thought of as a murderer."

"He certainly frightens me," sniffed Quentin.

You're not the only one," said Arthur, "there's a lot of people around 'ere who are scared of Big Harry."

"Come along," said Queenie, "no time to chatter about Big Harry, you two get up to the hospital and collect Steve and Quentin and I will make sure everything is in place here."

"Pity about Mr Bland," said Arthur, "I don't suppose he'll come tomorrow. Perhaps Mrs Bland might come."

Perhaps," said Teddy, "It would be nice if she did."

Chapter Forty-Seven
Andrew's Visit

Jean and the boys had their lunch and Jean sent them to the supermarket with a list, to do the weekend shopping. She told them to stick to the list if possible and not to buy any silly things.

"As she sat there quietly sipping a cup of coffee she heard a light tap on the front door. That's odd she thought why didn't they ring the bell nobody would hear a tap like that. It was almost as though the person outside was checking to see if the house was occupied. Jean knew who it was, Bland had told her to expect a visit.

She moved silently down the hall and whipped open the front door. There stood Andrew Middleton with a bunch of skeleton keys in his hand, which he hastily put in his pocket.

"Mrs Bland," he said surprised, "I wasn't sure that you would be in, I thought you might be at the hospital."

"Well," said Jean smiling, "It's lucky for you that I'm not, please come in." Andrew stepped inside. Jean knew full well that he had been hoping that she and the boys were out so he could let himself in.

"What can I do for you?" said Jean as she led him up the hall.

"Well its nothing really," said Andrew, I'm not sure that you can help."

"Try me," said Jean.

"Well Robert has some paperwork that he's been looking after for me. It's to do with a case and I need it back."

"Ah," said Jean, "you mean the black book and the reports. Robert said you might be calling in for them. Come along upstairs and we'll get them now."

"When they reached the attic Jean brought the little leather case out of her pocket and handed it to Andrew.

She watched as he unscrewed the carvings and let the panel down. He dropped the book and papers into a document case he was holding and handed the wallet back to Jean. Jean opened the wallet and saw that the screwdriver and the special key were missing.

"Oh Andrew," she said, "I think you must have accidentally dropped the key and screwdriver in your bag. Before Andrew could zip up the bag Jean had grabbed it and emptied the contents on the floor.

"Ah there they are," she said retrieving them from among the scattered papers. She put them back in the wallet and tucked it deep down in her pocket.

"Lets me help you," said Jean kneeling down to help Andrew collect up the papers.

"No Mrs Bland, I'll do I, there are some really dreadful photos among these papers and Robert would never forgive me if you accidentally saw any of them." He scooped everything up and stuffed them into the bag as quickly as possible.

"Would you care for some tea," said Jean sweetly.

"No thanks," said Andrew, "I have to get back with these papers the powers that be are anxious for their return. Robert did really well you know."

"I do know," said Jean, "and I'm going to try and persuade him to retire."

"Surely not," said Andrew shocked, "he's so good at his job. What would he do?"

"I'm sure he'd think of something," said Jean.

"What would you live on?"

"We'd manage."

"Well must go," said Andrew opening the front door, "I'll pop in and see Robert, probably tomorrow."

"He'd like that," said Jean, "Good-bye."

"Bye," said Andrew as he walked up the drive. Jean noticed that he had parked the car well out of sight from the road. She closed the front door and leaned against it. He had obviously hoped to find the house empty, that's why he had the skeleton keys. Robert was right he really was a secret squirrel. Tonight she would have to have a straight talk with Robert, there was something she must tell him.

Chapter Forty-Eight
Confession Time.

When Jean and the boys arrived to visit Bland ,Giles was packing to go home. The doctor had given him the green light.

"Perhaps I'll see some of you at the opening tomorrow," said Giles.

"Perhaps," said Jean.

"Cheerio," said Giles and picked up his gear and left.

"Boys," said Jean, "could you go up to the canteen and get some coffee?"

"Sure," said Seth, "come on David."

"Oh well all right," said David grudgingly.

As they went down the corridor David said,

"Why are we going to get coffee when we've already had some?"

"Because Jean needs to speak to Robert alone. Really David sometimes you're so insensitive to other people's feelings. You cant see what's right in front of you. We'll take it slowly and not hurry back. We can look around the little shop there,"

"Right," said David.

Robert looked pale and tired.

"Jean I want you to go to the opening tomorrow, I promised them we'd all go. I've reserved and paid for some miniatures for you. Teddy will give them to you."

"Robert I have something to tell you before the boys get back. I'm seriously rich."

"That's nice," said Bland,

"No you don't understand I mean seriously, seriously rich. Archie never trusted banks although he had two really good pensions in place for us. All through our married life he bought diamonds once a month in Amsterdam, what ever he could afford. They are all registered in little envelopes. It's all *bone fide* none of them were bought with ill-gotton gains. They can all be matched against his salary. The company that he bought them from is Van Haydons a very prestigious company. I had a letter from them six months ago saying if all the diamonds that we had purchased from them were still in my possession that would be worth a lot of money. I didn't know about them until after his death,"

Bland stared at Jean

"How much," he croaked

"A conservative estimate would be approximately seventy-five million pounds sterling. But they would have to be checked."

"HOW MUCH," shouted Bland giving himself a pain in his side.

"About seventy-five million."

"That's what I thought you said."

"You see Robert we don't have to worry about money. You could retire"

"Indeed I could,"

"Will you?"

"No."

"Ah well," Jean sighed, "you can't blame me for trying." David and Seth came back with the coffees

"Here we are," said Seth handing them around.

"Thanks," said Jean, "Robert wants us to go to the opening tomorrow, what do you think David?"

"Yes sure, " said David.

"Good," said Bland, "you can all come and tell me all about it tomorrow night. Now take your coffees and go home, I'm feeling very tired and my side's hurting."

When they got outside David wanted to know why they were going when basically they had only just arrived.

"He really is poorly," said Jean, "and I told him about the diamonds."

"No wonder," laughed David, "that must have shocked him."

"Diamonds, what diamonds?" asked Seth.

"I'll tell you some other time," said David.

After they had gone Bland assessed the situation. He felt like shit and he wasn't sure if he had popped one of his stitches. Maybe Jean was right, perhaps he should retire. He seemed to be getting hurt a lot lately. He must be slowing up. He was sorry to be missing the opening tomorrow, but Jean and the boys would be able to have a good time. He wouldn't be missed. Presently the nurse came in and gave him something for the pain and to help him sleep. After a while he drifted away on a euphoric cloud as the drug took effect.

Chapter Forty-Nine
The Opening

Everybody at the Galleries was dressed up and ready to go. Quentin looked great in his black. His shirt was snowy white and his bow tie was tied to perfection. He wore plain steel framed glasses, no stars, no diamante and Queenie, Teddy and Arthur were really proud of him.

" You look the real biz," said Arthur.

"We all do, " said Teddy, "Don't you look good Queenie?"

"Well said Queenie, I thought I'd splash out on something new."

She was wearing her usual black, but the dress was long and flowing with a long flowing coat over the top, both were decorated in black shiny beads.

"You look really good," said Arthur, "better than that tight stuff that you usually wear that makes you bum look big, don't 'ardly notice your bum in that outfit."

" I'll thank you not to mention my posterior," said Queenie in an offended tone, It's not the thing that a real gentleman would do."

"I 'ain't no gentleman," said Arthur, "there's no two ways about that."

Queenie stomped off and went to check her gowns.

"Don't go upsetting 'er," said Teddy, "not this early in the day."

Big Harry and his wife turned up an hour before the opening as promised. His wife looked as though she was going to Ascot. She was wearing a hugh pink, wide hat with masses of silk roses on it. It matched the pink frilly long dress she was wearing, also with lots of pink roses on the shoulders and cascading down the dress and around the hem. To top it all she was wearing a white fox fur stole.

Quite a crowd had gathered and Giles was busy taking photographs. Big Harry made a rather embarrassing speech, mostly about himself and his place in the community, the ribbon was cut, much to everybody's relief, and Big Harry's wife was presented with a large bouquet of flowers. The jazz band started up and the champagne started to flow. The ladies made straight for the gown shop, in fact there was a lot of squealing and some polite pushing and shoving.

Jean was amazed how beautiful the gowns looked, Amanda grabbed a pale blue creation which she wouldn't let go of and sent Boyd to get Queenie so that she could pay for it and take it to the car, safe in the boot where the other females couldn't see it.

Jean and the boys went to the furniture and Jean purchased the antique Italian mirror and the chandelier. Then they went to visit Steve in the Art Gallery. The place was heaving with customers. Teddy gave her the miniatures that Bland had purchased for her and she also purchased four more miniatures of orchids and two larger paintings that Steve had done in Australia when they all went out on a visit there.

"Look Mrs Bland," said Teddy, "I'll bring everything round to your 'ouse tomorrow. Give me the miniatures and I'll put them in a safe place."

"Thanks Teddy," said Jean.

"Now," said Teddy, "go and get yourselves somefing to eat and drink, there's some tables and chairs over there, go and 'ave a good time."

They did have a very good time, they chatted to Steve and sat at a table with Frenchie and Florentine talking about the oncoming wedding. Giles was also having a good time; he was taking pictures of happy people for a change. His new paper was delighted with him, and he had a steady income again, and best of all Jessica had been avenged at last.

Jean, David and Seth left early as Seth wanted to see Bland before he flew to America and David was taking him to the airport.

Bland was sitting up in bed looking a lot better and he was having a light meal. They had cut it up for him as he could only use one arm, due to the wounds in his shoulder and in his side his other arm was in a sling to keep it as still as possible.

They all started talking at once telling him about the opening.

"It was a success then?" said Bland.

"Oh yes," said Jean, "the food was delicious."

"And the champagne," said David.

"They had a jazz band and balloons and I believe there are going to be fireworks later in the evening."

"How do you feel about inheriting two sons?" asked David.

"Love it," said Bland; "I hope your going to take good care of us in our dotage."

"Only two visitors per person," said the nurse as she bustled in.

"We're going," said Seth, "got to get to the airport."

They said their good-byes and left, leaving Jean And Bland alone.

"I think I'm going to put in for a spot of leave," said Bland, "where would you like to go?"

"Singapore," said Jean, "I'd love to go there."

"Singapore it is then," said Bland. "I need to get better first, and we have got Frenchie and Florentines wedding to go to."

"I'm looking forward to that," said Jean, we were chatting to them today, they are such a lovely couple as so in love, even after all these years."

* * * * * *

On the way to the airport David realised how much he was going to miss Seth. As they went to the check-in counter David said,

"You will keep in touch wont you?"

"Yes," said Seth.

"Text or call me when you arrive."

"I will."

Seth handed his passport and tickets to the girl and answered a few questions. He only had hand luggage with him as his costumes and belongings had already been shipped the previous week. He turned to David and said,

I might as well go straight through David, there's no sense in you hanging about." He tucked his passport and boarding card in his pocket.

"Okay," said David,

"Good luck David."

"And you."

"Seth," called David as Seth turned to go through the gate. I'll always be here for you."

"Thank-you David, I've always been there for you, ever since I came to live with you and Jean. Good-bye," and he turned, walked through the gate and was gone. Walking away from David was the hardest thing he ever had to do.

David slowly walked out of the airport. He could not believe that Seth felt something for him, and now he was gone. Well thought David, I shall be gone next week. Maybe I might be able to travel from the coast and see Seth at Las Vegas. America is a big place and David did not know how far apart they were going to be.

Chapter Fifty
Visits

Teddy was as good as his word; all four of them arrived dead on nine the next morning with Jean's purchases. Teddy and Arthur hung the mirror under strict supervision from Quentin. Next they hung the chandelier and the paintings. The paintings were moved about quite a bit until Quentin was completely satisfied. They had coffee with Jean and left telling her that they were going to visit Mr Bland.

After their departure, Jean started Sunday lunch. David was extremely quiet.

"Something wrong?" enquired Jean.

"No," said David.

"I suppose you're missing Seth."

"I'm okay," said David, "I'll go and set the table."

"Very well Dear, said Jean. David drifted into the dining room and later Jean could hear him playing his guitar in his bedroom. He was playing the blues.

* * * * * *

Bland was lying in his bed looking at the ceiling. The doctor had come and gone and he had suggested that Bland might spend some time out of bed the next day, Meanwhile he wanted him to rest before lunch, take a little nap. Bland was bored, now that Giles was gone he had the room to himself, there was no one to talk to. He heard people talking in the corridor and the doors crashed open and the fabulous four burst in.

Hello Mr Bland," said Quentin, thought we'd pop in to visit you." They had brought flowers, chocolate and grapes. The all got chairs and settled around the bed.

"We didn't bring Steve," said Teddy, "we left him in bed resting as he's only been out of hospital for two days." Queenie opened the box of chocolates, found the coffee cream and popped it into Bland's mouth.

"There you are Mr Bland, I know it's your favourite." They chatted about the opening and Bland was happy just to lie there and listen to them. It seemed that Big Harry made a big show of buying furniture for his 'London home'. He unrolled a wad of cash and peeled off the notes so that every body could see. His wife found a dress that fitted her, not one of Jean's, and she bought hats and bags. Queenie sold half her stock, mostly Jean's gowns.

Steve's paintings and miniatures went very well. He was amazed and gratified by how much people liked his work. Practically all the miniatures were sold. Teddy told him to put his prices up as he felt he was selling them much too cheaply.

Teddy had told him to think how much they charge up west. The furniture department had also done well; there was always a ready market for really good pieces. Omar's father had bought the Persian carpets and was very pleased indeed as one was very rare and he was keeping it for himself. He was now Teddy and Arthur's new best friend.

Lots of champagne was drunk and Teddy said that you could have fed the third world on the amount of food that was consumed. All in all it had been a very good day.

Suddenly the nurse appeared, large and threatening.

"What's all this?" she demanded, "and how did you get in?"

"On our legs," said Arthur, "we come to see our mate Mr Bland."

"Detective Chief Inspector Bland is supposed to be sleeping. He is not well as you can plainly see," she said, "and pray what is all this mess?"

"We brought him a few sweeties," said Queenie.

"So I can see," said the nurse surveying the chocolate wrappings and grape stalks and pips all over the bed. There was a long tatty stalk with just three grapes on it, all that was left, none eaten by Bland. All he had had was the one chocolate that Queenie had given him.

The nurse went to the door and shouted 'nurse' down the corridor and a young nurse came running.

"There's no need to run nurse," she said, "now please clear up this mess. The chief Inspector's lunch will be served in about five minutes time.

She wrested the box of chocolates away from Queenie's fierce grasp, put on the lid and placed it on the bedside cupboard. The young nurse collected up all the rubbish in a plastic bag and went off to dispose of it.

Now," said the nurse, "I must ask you to leave. There is never more than two visitors at any one time and I would be pleased if you would kindly remember that on your next visit."

They said their good-byes and departed, promising to come back soon. Bland could hear Arthur as he went down the corridor, his words echoing back.

"Pan faced old cow, bet she's not getting any." There was the slight raising of one eyebrow to show that the nurse had heard him. The young nurse came back and the two of the adjusted Bland's bed into a sitting position.

"Now Inspector as you didn't have your rest this morning, I think you had better have it this afternoon."

"Oh no thought Bland I've got to get better, and soon, I can't stand this place.

Later in the afternoon Jean came in to see him and he was allowed to sit up.

"No David then?"

"No," said Jean, "He's moping."

"I guess he's missing Seth."

"I think he does, but he won't admit it."

"Well it's opened his eyes," said Bland.

"I hope so," said Jean, "Robert how well do you know Andrew?

"As well as you can know those secret types." Jean told him about Andrew's visit and how he tried to take the keys.

"I'm sure he was going to break in, his car was hidden out of sight of the road and he had skeleton keys."

"Don't doubt it for one minute," said Bland, "did you know that minder sat next to the bed every night and I knew nothing about it?"

"How would he get past the big iron key you need for the front door?"

"Probably had one made up, the other two locks he could open with skeleton keys."

"Well I think that it's really sneaky."

"It's what he does best."

"Oh well," said Jean, "if your not worried then why should I."

"I'm hoping to get out by the week-end, so I can go to the wedding."

"Oh Robert that would be lovely, but will they let you?"

"Well the wounds don't look too bad, they are not infected, so I'm hoping for the best."

"Robert those miniatures were lovely. Thank-you so much."

"I'm glad you like them."

"I bought other things too."

"I know Teddy and the gang came to visit this morning, and he said that you had bought a few bits and pieces although he didn't say what. They got thrown out by the nurse." Jean laughed.

"They brought those lovely flowers, a box of chocolates and some grapes. They ate all the grapes and I had one chocolate. The nurse took the box away from Queenie and put it on the cupboard. Queenie looked really put out as she'd only managed to eat one layer, and hung on to the box as long as she could, but the nurse was stronger and managed to get it away from her."

They chatted on until the nurse came in and said it was time to go. Jean left and Bland settled down to another boring night.

Chapter Fifty-One
Monday

Monday morning came and Boyd was sitting in the Super's office.

"It's like this Boyd, the court case against the Oates has been brought forward and as Robert is in hospital you will have to go on your own. You have all the information ready don't you."

"I do Sir but I wish Mr Bland could be there I don't want those two to weasel out of it. I'm not good under cross examination."

"You'll be fine Boyd, Just speak up and tell the truth, don't let their counsel put words into your mouth. Pop along and see Robert if you want to, if I know him, he'll be fed up to the back teeth by now and would welcome a bit of distraction. He'll give you a few pointers.

Did you hear about Colin Jeeves? He's been arrested this morning, and about time too. Oh yes, all the arseholes are going down like flies. I always disliked him; I felt that he was bent. It quite made my day when I heard that he was arrested. Well off you go to the hospital. Take your files and consult with Robert, Pop in and see me tomorrow."

"Yes Sir, said Boyd, and he made a quick exit. He didn't like court cases, they were mostly long and boring, but he would be glad to se the Oates go down. He made sure he had some change for the hospital car park and left the building before anyone else could find him a job.

Bland was pleased to see him. Boyd thought he looked pale but at least he didn't have all those tubes sticking out of him. He just had the one drip bag and he was due to have that removed later.

They spent a good part of the morning talking over the case and planning strategy. The nurse wasn't happy with Boyd's presence. She thought the hospital would function much better without the complications of patients and visitors, however he did not seem to be tiring the Inspector, in fact the opposite. He told Boyd that he wished he could attend, as he'd like to see the Oates get what they deserved.

"I wish you were there too Sir. When do you think they are going to let you out?"

"No idea Boyd, but I'd like to be out by the wedding on Sunday."

"That would be great," said Boyd.

"Has the Super mentioned anything about the Messenger case?"

"No nothing, he's enjoying the downfall of Colin Jeeves and all the other coppers that he suspected of being bent. He's in a good mood at the moment. He's been on television and in the papers, he's quite the hero of the hour, and you too Sir being stabbed by La Roche in the performance of your duty."

"Really," said Bland, "does it mention that I was rescued from La Roche by a fellow officer killing him? I bet it doesn't say that. The secret squirrels all go back to their hiding places. The Super gets the kudos and life goes on. Everything slips back into place, and in a fortnight everyone will have forgotten all about it."

"You think so Sir?"

"I know so Boyd."

"Detective Chief Inspector Bland," said the nurse, "it's time for your lunch, your visitor must go."

Boyd jumped up and picked up his files,

" I'll come and see you tomorrow Sir, after the trial if I can. Hopefully it won't run into the next day."

"Good," said Bland, "I look forward to it."

"Bye, Sir," said Boyd and he disappeared through the swing doors.

"Now," said Bland turning his attention to the nurse, "what culinary delights have we to tickle our palette today?"

"I'm sure I don't know," said the nurse, "that is not my concern. I would guess that it will be something cold." Bland's heart sank when it came it looked like a very watery stew, bits of carrot, several small pieces of potato and two extra small pieces unidentifiable meat. They must have an electron microscope in that kitchen to cut it so small thought Bland. It was all swimming in orange coloured gravy. Bland softly hummed 'sweet mystery of life at last I've found you' and took a tentative mouthful. Fortunately it was completely tasteless and he managed to get it down, he then ate the sweet, which seemed to consist of shaving foam and pink rubber. The nurse seemed very pleased. Bland hoped that his next visitor would bring him some real food.

Halfway through the afternoon Andrew popped in.

"Good to see you Andrew," said Bland.

"Sorry my man didn't get to you sooner."

"Nonsense," said Bland, "he couldn't help it, at least he rescued me in the end."

"All the same I'm not happy about it," said Andrew frowning.

"You can't change it Andrew, so don't beat yourself up."

"Where's that old crab apple of a nurse?"

"She's gone for her late lunch, won't be back for a while."

"Good I've brought you two unofficial visitors, I'll go and get them."

When he came back he had Dave from 'The Chippy' and his little girl with him.

"As you couldn't get to see them, I've brought them to you." The little girl looked very pale but seemed none the worse for her experience.

"Thank's Mr Bland," said Dave, "I can't tell you enough 'ow grateful I am. Me and the wife are so 'appy now that we've got our little girl back."

"It's was your doing Dave, you told me where to find the lists, and Andrew here was responsible for the actual rescue."

"But you were the one who went after the lists, where others would be too scared to try it. You were the one who nearly lost his life," said Dave.

"Well you're welcome," said Bland.

"Say thank-you to Mr Bland Charlotte."

"Fank-you Mr Bland," whispered Charlotte and she then hid behind her father's legs.

"She's a bit shy," said Dave.

"How are you feeling now Dave?" enquired Bland.

"Oh I'm in the pink now that I've got my baby back. What do a few bruises matter. My wife is over the moon; she can't stop crying at the moment, I suppose it's the relief."

"Give her my best," said Bland.

"I will do Mr. Bland, I suppose we had better go before that old dragon of a nurse gets back. Don't forget where to come for your fish and chips, on the 'ouse, your money won't be any good in our establishment, my wife will see to that. Good bye Mr Bland."

As he was going out the nurse came in, and she did not look best pleased

"It's time for the Inspector to have his afternoon rest," she said frostily.

"Well cheerio Robert, come and spend some time down on the estate, you and Jean, let Mrs Mannering pamper you both, she's good at that. Have a bit of piece and quiet where no one can get at you." He glared at the nurse and left.

Later in the evening when Jean arrived he mentioned it to her.

"What's the place like?" said Jean.

"Wonderful, I've been there before, all their food is home grown, he has a big farm, and it's very luxurious."

"Then we'll go," said Jean, "at least you won't be working, and also he can break into our house when ever it suits him."

They both laughed.

Chapter Fifty-Two
A Day in Court

Boyd sat against the wall down the side of the court. He was one of the arresting officers and would be called to give evidence.

He looked around the court, the defendants were in the dock, and probably the cleanest they had ever been. Daily showers and a haircut made both of them look better.

Bland had always said that the law was there to serve the law, it had nothing to do with justice, and in his life he had tried to redress the balance. He reckoned that the courts and its proceedings were pure theatre and he would have certainly have enjoyed today's performance.

The Oates could not see that they had done anything wrong. As far as they were concerned they were the victims..

The court was packed and several times they jeered at the Oates. The judge banged his gavel done very rapidly and hard and said that if they did it again he would clear the court.

They denied starving Beth saying that she only had a small apatite and because Johnny's back was bad he could not work, so therefore did not have any money, and he did not go on the social because he had his pride. The spectators booed once more and the judge threatened them once more and brought the court to order.

"No," said the prosecuting counsel drawing himself to his full height, aware that he had a willing and appreciative audience,

"You did not go to the local authority, because you were signed on with four other authorities, under six other names and if what those authorities tell us is true you were receiving a sizable income from them". A round of cheering and clapping broke out and the counsel almost bowed to his audience, and the red-faced judge had all the spectators removed from the court.

At the end of the day they had many charges against them, ill treatment, gross neglect and cruelty to a child, likely to cause her death, fraud on a grand scale, housebreaking, grievous bodily harm. People had come forward after he had been locked up and could no longer get at them. They had hospital photos of their injuries and enough evidence against him, to put him away for a long time. The jury took five minutes to find them guilty and they were remanded, waiting to be sentenced the following week, when it would be decided how long the sentences should be.

The judge said they were a menace to society and should not be allowed on the streets again, so that good people could rest easy in their beds knowing they were locked up and could do them no harm.

Boyd reported back to Bland, who was pleased with the result.

"The Super's ecstatic, he's giving another press conference tomorrow morning. He's so puffed up with pride."

"Pride goes before a fall," muttered Bland.

"Any thoughts on the Messenger case Boyd?"

"No Sir, what about you?"

"No," said Bland, "But like I said before I'm sure I know something in the back of my head. At least we've had no more murders."

"Don't temp providence by mentioning it Sir," said Boyd.

On Thursday David flew to America. Jean went to the airport to see him off and then spent more of her time at the hospital with Bland.

As the week went past he seemed to be improving fast. He was allowed up now and spent most of his day in a wheelchair. He could get down to the canteen and Jean wheeled him around the garden at the back of the hospital.

The hospital agreed that he might go to the wedding but he would have to return, as he wasn't well enough to go home yet. He would be allowed out at twelve mid-day and would have to be back by seven in the evening, earlier if possible, especially if he felt unwell. Jean hired a special van because of the wheelchair and she brought his wedding clothes to the hospital.

Chapter Fifty-Three
Frenchie and Florentine's Wedding

When the wedding day arrived it was clear and bright. There was a slight autumn chill in the air but the sun was warm. The church was filled with sweet smelling flowers, and the sun shone through the stained-glass windows and golden light filled with rainbows lit up the couple as they stood before the alter.

It was a beautiful wedding; Queenie, Quentin, Amanda and Jean shed a few tears.

Florentine was wearing a long lavender silk gown with long sleeves and a high collar. Her bouquet was made the old fashioned way with lots of flowers and ribbons cascading down her dress. Today people held small posies or a single flower. She walked very slowly as she suffered terrible with arthritis. Frenchie also walked slowly as he had aggressive pancreatic cancer and he wanted to marry his beloved Florentine before he had to go into the hospice. Like Florentine nothing could be done for him. Giles was here, there, and everywhere taking beautiful pictures.

After the wedding they all went back to Frenchie's place. Although it was an old house, Frenchie had had a lift installed and they all went up to the first floor above the shop. It was a huge room with deep bays and long Georgian windows, beautifully furnished, mostly French in style. A fire burned brightly in the large marble fireplace. The three tiered wedding cake was on it's own round table. Beautiful sugar flowers cascaded down the cake like a brightly coloured waterfall.

"Now my friends," said Frenchie, " I know it is not ze tradition but we are going to cut the cake first and Monsieur Giles can take some pictures and when zat is done we can all sit down togezzer, and enjoy our meal."

The cake was cut and everybody sat at the large round table. Frenchie had brought caterers in and the table was beautifully laid and decorated. Frenchie's silver gleamed in the candlelight given off by very large silver candelabra on the table and around the room.

Waitresses appeared from the kitchen and filled the champagne glasses.

"There are no speeches at zis wedding," said Frenchie, "all my beloved Florentine and I wish to say is welcome, and thank-you for coming." All the glasses were charged and Teddy called for a toast to the bride and groom. Frenchie and Florentine did not have champagne; they had small crystal goblets, the contents of which were a French raspberry liqueur, which Florentine had brought over from France.

"Thank-you from both of us," said Frenchie holding Florentine's small hand, "it is so good to be among friends, who are sharing our wedding day with us."

Frenchie requested that Bland's wheelchair be placed next to him, so that they could talk.

The first course was served, and the waitresses moved silently around filling glasses, and removing plates, and bringing fresh courses as required. People chatted happily, the fire crackled and the flickering candles gave a golden glow to the whole occasion.

"So my dear Inspector," said Frenchie, "they let you out for our wedding."

"Yes," said Bland, "but I have to go back this evening. I wouldn't have missed this for the world." Jean cut up his food as he could not use his arm properly yet.

"I was a leetle anxious that you might not come," said Frenchie.

"Really," said Bland, "I fully intended to come in spite of what the hospital might say. Jean has been really looking forward to it."

"I have a letter for you eet might be of use to you when you get back to work. Don't open it until then," he pushed the letter across the table.

"Very well," said Bland picking it up and tucking it into his inside pocket.

"Florentine and I have made out ze wills and have given them to Teddy for safe keeping. We 'as no family so we are leaving the premises to Quentin. Please do not say anything as he doesn't know yet."

"Not a word," said Bland, "you can rely on me."

"I am very sure of zat dear Inspector."

Eventually the coffee and brandy and liqueurs were served and the table was cleared and people went and sat on the couches to chat.

"Frenchie," shouted Teddy, "Do you have any more of that white china?"

"Yes my friend I picked up three nice pieces last week, go downstairs and have a look around, everybody go down and 'ave a look around. Quentin I purchased some very nice Italian glass the last time I went across ze channel why don't you go down and unpack it, you can see if there is anything that you like."

"Will you be alright Darling," said Jean, "I would love to have a look around."

"Of course he will be alright," said Frenchie, "he is with Florentine and I. He is among friends."

Everybody clattered excitedly down the stairs and could be heard calling to each other as they found things they liked. Only Florentine, Frenchie and Bland remained.

"Well," said Bland, "this has been a wonderful day."

"I am so glad that you enjoyed it my friend, it's a pity that I have to destroy it."

"What do you mean Frenchie?" said Bland feeling suddenly cold.

"Look at my beloved Florentine," Bland looked and saw that she was asleep. Tears flowed down Frenchie's face.

"You know that she 'as arthritis, she can barely walk. Getting up the aisle was the pain most tremendous. Painkillers seem to 'ave no effect. Her bladder is very weak and she suffers from incontinence, which is awful for someone so pristine and pure as she is. She has a delicate elegance that I have seen in no other woman. I have to buckle on her shoes. as her hands are so swollen and weak that she cannot manage. Even carrying her flowers was agonising for her. Today I dressed her hair and helped her on wiz her gown."

"She looks beautiful," said Bland.

"I myself 'ave ze cancer of the pancreas and it 'as invaded other parts of my body. Very soon I will 'ave to go into ze hospice. As with Florentine death is our only option."

"What are you telling me Frenchie?" said Bland feeling a cold hand clutching at his heart.

"I am telling you my friend that Florentine is dead, and I am about to join her. The toast you know, the raspberry liqueur disguised ze bitter taste of ze drug. We agreed that this was to be our last day on ze earth,"

Bland looked at Florentine and she looked so peaceful, there was no pain in her face. Bland stared at her and then he noticed the crystal beads around her neck and her wrist. My God he thought that's what I saw in Frenchie's shop, the something that he could not remember – crystal beads and a little

French doll. The same beads that Beth had been wearing when they found her, with her little French doll and teddy.

"You're the Messenger of Death," whispered Bland.

"Yes," said Frenchie, "I do not regret it, and I 'ope that I will be forgiven. He told the silent Bland about the other deaths and what had happened. The letter he had given him was his confession. He told Bland a few other things and then he closed his hand over Florentine's, closed his eyes, and whispered *au revoir* and was gone.

Bland sat there in the silence. He felt really alone now; the fire crackled and the candles made long alien shadows on the walls, it was getting dark now. The whole mood had changed. Bland leaned back in the wheelchair, it was as though he was in a kind of surreal dream. His eyes wanted to cry. He could hear the others downstairs laughing and happy, and he wanted to call them but couldn't. Please he thought, someone come soon I can't bear it.

Chapter Fifty-Four
Finally

A couple of weeks later Bland left hospital and went home. He seemed to have sunk into a deep depression. Jean spoke to Andrew and it was arranged for them to go to his estate. Jean wanted him to be away from work and away from home where people from work could get at him.

The Messenger of Death case was sorted out, Frenchie leaving a confession helped. Before they went to Andrew's Bland and Jean went to Frenchie and Florentine's funerals. Teddy had all arranged it all. It was a green funeral they were buried in a field, no flowers and no headstone. The wild grasses and flowers would grow over their graves and eventually it would become a conservation area. They would be forgotten, except by their friends. Willy the cyclist's parents attended and laid a wreath with a card which said,

SAY HELLO TO WILLY FOR US. WE FORGIVE YOU AND MAY YOU REST IN PEACE.

After a couple of weeks on the estate Bland got restless and they returned home. Jean had a small dinner party for Bland and invited Boyd and Amanda.

That evening Bland seemed to be back to his old self again. They talked about La Roche and the Oates and finally about Frenchie And Florentine.

"So sad, said Jean

"I agree," said Amanda.

"Do you know the last thing that Frenchie said to me?" said Bland.

They all looked at him and shook their heads.

"He said, "You know Chief Inspector, it really was Murder Most Beautiful."

About the Author

The author was born in the Medway Valley in Kent and was brought up there during the war years. She still lives in Kent with her husband in the old Medieval town of Faversham. She came to writing late in life after the family had left home and she had retired. She writes both for children and adults, and her childrens books have the element of magic and adventure, and her adult books have mystery and intrigue. She writes for the nine year old in all of us, as she believes that we all need a little bit of mystery and magic in our lives.

Lightning Source UK Ltd.
Milton Keynes UK
23 March 2010

151759UK00001B/40/P